Read Me a Story

This is the book for every parent who is wise
enough to realise that a child's start in life largely
depends on how quickly he is introduced to the
reading habit. Some of the contents will be enjoyed
by three year olds, much more by four and five
year olds; and all by six year olds. How quickly
the child begins to read the contents for himself is
another matter, for this depends greatly on the
patience and skill of the parents. But it will be very
surprising indeed if the time lag is too noticeable.

This, then, is a book for children *and* parents to
enjoy. There is no Reading Scheme here, no con-
trolled vocabulary, no science at all — just the
magic of old and new story-tellers who can set a
child's imagination alight.

Read Me a Story

A collection of stories and
verse for the young

Selected and edited by
Frank Waters

Beaver Books

First published in 1974
under the title *Reading with Mother* by
George G. Harrap & Company Limited
182–184 High Holborn, London WC1V 7AX

This paperback edition published in 1976 by
The Hamlyn Publishing Group Limited
London · New York · Sydney · Toronto
Astronaut House, Feltham, Middlesex, England
Third impresssion 1979

© Copyright George G. Harrap & Company Limited 1974
ISBN 0 600 37580 3

Printed in England by
Cox & Wyman Limited
London, Reading and Fakenham
Set in Baskerville

Foreword

The aim of this volume is quite simple. It is to provide a collection of stories and poetry, a high proportion of which is guaranteed to amuse and entertain any child who has begun to read, and welcomes encouragement. The age of the child will of course vary, but it must be obvious from the selection of the largely traditional material that it is expected to be under seven.

I am glad to make the following acknowledgements in respect of copyright material.

To The Literary Trustees of Walter de la Mare and the Society of Authors as their representative for *The Wolf and the Fox* by Walter de la Mare

To Thomas Nelson and Sons Ltd for *The First Pike* from *Old Peter's Russian Tales* by Arthur Ransome

To Mrs George Bainbridge and the Macmillan Company of London and Basingstoke for *How the Camel got its Hump* from *Just So Stories* by Rudyard Kipling

To the Estate of A. A. Milne for *Bad Sir Brian Botany* from *When We Were Very Young* by A. A. Milne (and also to the Canadian publishers, McClelland and Stewart Ltd, Toronto)

To Gerald Duckworth and Co. Ltd for *Matilda* from *Cautionary Verses* by Hilaire Belloc

To George G. Harrap and Co. Ltd for the work of Joyce Lankester Brisley and Modwena Sedgwick

To the Macmillan Company of London and Basingstoke for the illustrations by Harry Furniss from *Sylvie and Bruno* by Lewis Carroll.

Finally I mention the little versions of *The Tale of the Turnip* and *The Three Pigs*, which were written for me by Olive Gayford shortly before her tragic death. They were written as part of another project but their inclusion here, with the approval of her friend Miss Carr, gives me an opportunity of paying some small tribute to the memory of a most remarkable personality: a teacher of rare quality and one who inspired the greatest respect and affection.

F.W.

Contents

Henny-Penny

There was once a great big chestnut tree growing in a field where a lot of hens and chickens lived. One day a little yellow chicken called Chicky-Wicky was standing under the tree, and a prickly green chestnut fell *plop* on to her back.

'Oh,' thought Chicky-Wicky, 'the sky is falling! I must run and tell everyone!'

So she ran, and she ran, until she met a pretty speckled hen called Henny-Penny.

'Henny-Penny,' cried Chicky-Wicky, all out of breath, 'I feel *so* excited, the sky is tumbling down! A piece of it fell on my back just now!'

'We must let the King know about this at once,' returned Henny-Penny.

So she and Chicky-Wicky ran, and ran, until they met Ducky-Wucky.

'Ducky-Wucky,' cried Henny-Penny, 'the sky is tumbling down — a piece of it fell on Chicky-Wicky's back just now — and we're going to tell the King.'

'I'm coming too,' said Ducky-Wucky.

8

And the three birds ran, and ran, till they met Goosey-Woosey.

'Goosey-Woosey,' cried Henny-Penny, 'the sky is tumbling down — a piece of it fell on Chicky-Wicky's back — and we're all on our way to tell the King about it.'

'I'm coming too,' said Goosey-Woosey.

And the four birds ran, and ran, until they met Turkey-Wurkey.

'Turkey-Wurkey,' cried Henny-Penny, 'haven't you heard the news? The sky is tumbling down — a great big piece of it fell on Chicky-Wicky's back — and we are on our way to let the King know about it.'

'I'm coming too,'. said Turkey-Wurkey.

And the five birds ran, and ran, till they met Foxy-Woxy.

'Foxy-Woxy,' cried Henny-Penny, 'the sky is tumbling down — a great big piece fell on Chicky-Wicky just now — and we all on our way to tell the King about it!'

'Dear me,' said Foxy-Woxy, 'I am sure his Majesty will be much interested. Do you know where he lives?'

'Oh, yes,' said Henny-Penny, 'he lives in a silver castle with a roof of gold!'

'Oh, no,' returned Foxy-Woxy, 'not at all — you are *quite* mistaken, Henny-Penny. He lives in a beautiful palace underground. I often go to see him there. So I know the way well.'

'Oh, do show *us* the way!' cried the five birds.

'With pleasure,' said Foxy-Woxy, smiling under his red whiskers. 'It's quite near here. All you have to do is to keep close behind me, and follow where I lead.'

So the five birds and Foxy-Woxy ran, and ran, till they came to Foxy-Woxy's own deep hole in the side of the hill.

'This is the way,' said Foxy-Woxy; and Chicky-Wicky, and Henny-Penny, and Ducky-Wucky, and Goosey-Woosey, and Turkey-Wurkey all kept close behind him, and followed where he led, as he had told them to.

And Foxy-Woxy led them into his own deep hole in the side of the hill, and I am sorry to say that not one of them ever came out again.

The Three Bears

Once upon a time there were Three Bears, who lived together in a house of their own, in a wood. One of them was a Little, Small, Wee Bear; and one was a Middle-sized Bear; and the other was a Great, Huge Bear. They had each

a bowl for their porridge; a little bowl for the Little, Small, Wee Bear; and a middle-sized bowl for the Middle Bear; and a big bowl for the Great, Huge Bear. And they each had a chair to sit in; a little chair for the Little, Small, Wee Bear; and a middle-sized chair for the Middle Bear; and a big chair for the Great, Huge Bear. And they each had a bed to sleep in; a little bed for the Little, Small, Wee Bear; a middle-sized bed for the Middle Bear; and a big bed for the Great, Huge Bear.

One day, after they had made the porridge for their breakfast, and poured it into their bowls, the Three Bears went into the wood while the porridge cooled, as they didn't want to burn their mouths by eating it too hot. While they were out a little girl, named Goldilocks, came up to the house. First she looked in at the window, and then she peeped in at the door; and then, seeing nobody about, she pushed the door wide open and went in.

Goldilocks felt very hungry, for she had come a long way, and when she saw the bowls of porridge on the table, she thought that she must taste some. First she picked up the big spoon belonging to the Great, Huge Bear, and tasted some of his porridge out of his great, big bowl — but it was

too hot for her. Then she picked up the middle-sized spoon belonging to the Middle Bear and tasted some of his porridge out of the middle bowl — but it was too cold for her. So she picked up the little spoon belonging to the Little, Small, Wee Bear and tasted some of his porridge out of his little bowl — and that was neither too hot nor too cold, but just right. So she ate it all up.

Then little Goldilocks, who was feeling tired, sat down in the chair belonging to the Great, Huge Bear — but it was too hard for her. Then she sat down in the chair belonging to the Middle Bear — but it was too soft for her. So she sat down in the chair belonging to the Little, Small, Wee Bear — and that was neither too hard nor too soft, but just right.

THE THREE BEARS

And she stayed there till the bottom of the chair came out and she sat down hard, on the floor.

After that, little Goldilocks went upstairs into the Bears' bedroom. First she lay down on the bed belonging to the Great, Huge Bear — but it was too high at the head for her. Next she lay down on the bed belonging to the Middle Bear, but it was too high at the foot for her. Then she lay down on the bed belonging to the Little, Small, Wee Bear — and that was neither too high at the head nor at the foot, but just right. So she pulled the clothes up over her and fell fast asleep.

By this time the Three Bears thought that their porridge would be cool enough to eat, so they came home for breakfast. Now, little Goldilocks had left the big spoon belonging to the Great, Huge Bear standing in his porridge, and when they got inside he saw it.

'SOMEBODY HAS BEEN EATING MY PORRIDGE!'

said the Great, Huge Bear in his great, gruff voice.

Then the Middle Bear looked at his bowl and saw that his spoon was standing in it, too, where Goldilocks had left it.

'SOMEBODY HAS BEEN EATING MY PORRIDGE!' said the Middle Bear, in his middle voice.

Then the Little, Small, Wee Bear looked at his bowl, and there was the spoon in it, but the porridge was all gone.

'SOMEBODY HAS BEEN EATING MY PORRIDGE, AND HAS EATEN IT ALL UP!' said the Little, Small, Wee Bear, in his little, small, wee voice.

Then the Three Bears began to look round to see if they could find who it was who had eaten the Little, Small, Wee Bear's breakfast. Now there was a hard cushion on the chair belonging to the Great. Huge Bear, and Goldilocks had not put it straight again when she got up.

'SOMEBODY HAS BEEN SITTING IN MY CHAIR!' said the Great, Huge Bear, in his great, gruff voice, when he saw it.

And Little Goldilocks had sat on the soft cushion on the chair belonging to the Middle Bear, and hadn't put it straight, either.

'SOMEBODY HAS BEEN SITTING IN MY CHAIR!' said the Middle Bear, in his middle voice.

And you know what Goldilocks had done to the chair belonging to the Little, Small, Wee Bear.

'SOMEBODY HAS BEEN SITTING IN MY CHAIR, AND HAS PUSHED THE BOTTOM OUT OF IT!' said the Little, Small, Wee Bear in his little, small, wee voice.

Then the Three Bears thought they would look round a bit more, so they went upstairs into their bedroom.

Now, little Goldilocks had pulled the pillow on the Great, Huge Bear's bed out of place, and when they came into the room he saw it.

THE THREE BEARS

'SOMEBODY HAS BEEN LYING IN MY BED!' said the Great, Huge Bear, in his great, gruff voice.

And little Goldilocks had pulled the pillow on the Middle Bear's bed out of place, and when he came in he saw it.

'SOMEBODY HAS BEEN LYING IN MY BED!' said the Middle Bear, in his middle voice.

And when the Little, Small, Wee Bear went over to look at his bed, there was the pillow in its place, but on the pillow was Goldilocks' golden head.

'SOMEBODY HAS BEEN LYING IN MY BED — AND HERE SHE IS!' said the Little, Small, Wee Bear in his little, small, wee voice.

Little Goldilocks had heard the great, gruff voice of the Great, Huge Bear, but she thought it was the wind in the trees. And she had heard the middle voice of the Middle Bear, but she thought it was someone speaking in a dream. But when she heard the little, small, wee voice of the Little, Small, Wee Bear, it was so sharp and shrill that it wakened her up at once.

She sat up and saw the Three Bears standing at one side of the bed looking at her. So she tumbled out at the other side and ran to the window, which was open, and jumped out. And that was the last that the Three Bears ever saw of little Goldilocks.

The Story of the Three Little Pigs

Three little pigs lived on a farm with mother and father pig. 'We are getting too big for this house,' said the first little pig, 'I wish I had a house to myself.'

'So do I,' said the second little pig.

'So do I,' said the third little pig.

'Let us go and make houses for ourselves.'

So the three little pigs set off.

The first little pig met a man. The man had a bundle of straw on his back.

'Will you please give me that straw? I am going to make a house so that I can live by myself,' said the little pig.

'Yes,' said the man, 'You can have my straw.'

'Thank you very much,' said the little pig and he took the straw and began to make a house.

He made the roof of straw

                the chimney of straw

                the walls of straw

                the windows of straw AND

                the door of straw.

Then the little pig went into the little straw house and shut the door.

The second little pig met a man with a lot of sticks on his back.

'Will you please give me your sticks? I am going to make a house so that I can live by myself,' said the little pig.

'Yes,' said the man, 'you can have my sticks.'

'Thank you very much,' said the little pig.

Then he began to make a house with the sticks.
He made the roof of sticks

        the chimney of sticks

        the walls of sticks

        the windows of sticks AND

        the door of sticks.

Then the little pig went into his stick house and shut the door.

The third little pig met a man with a lot of bricks on a cart.

'Will you please give me your bricks? I am going to make a house so that I can live by myself.'

'Yes,' said the man, 'you can have my bricks.'

'Thank you very much,' said the little pig, and he took the bricks and began to make his house.

He made the roof of bricks

        the chimney of bricks

        the walls of bricks BUT

        the door he made of sticks.

Then the little pig went into his brick house and shut the door.

The Big Bad Wolf was standing by a tree.

'I am going to eat the three little pigs,' he said to himself.

He went up to the little house of straw.

Rat - tat - tat!

'Little pig, little pig, let me in. Open the door and let me in,' he shouted.

'No, no, I will not open the door. I will not let you in,' said the little pig.

'Then I will huff and I will puff, and I will blow your house down,' said the Big Bad Wolf.

'You can huff and you can puff but I will not let you in,' said the little pig.

So the Big Bad Wolf huffed and he puffed and down fell the little straw house.

The little pig ran and ran. He ran to the little house of sticks.

'Let me in! Let me in!' he called out.

The little pig in the house of sticks let him in just as the Big Bad Wolf got up to the little house.

Rat - tat - tat!

'Little pigs, little pigs, let me in, Open the door and let me in!'

'No, no! We will not let you in,' they replied.

'Then I will huff and I will puff and I will blow your house down.'

'You can huff and you can puff but we will not open the door. We will not let you in.'

So the Big Bad Wolf huffed and he puffed and down fell the little house of sticks.

The little pigs ran and ran. They ran to the little house of bricks.

'Let us in! Let us in!' they called.

The little pig in the house of bricks let them in just as the Big Bad Wolf got up to the little house.

Rat - tat - tat!

'Little pigs, little pigs, let me in. Open the door. Do please let me in!'

'No, no. We will not let you in. We will not open the

door. We will not let you in,' said the three little pigs together.

'Then I will huff and I will puff and I will blow your house down!'

'You can huff and you can puff but we will not let you in.'

So the Big Bad Wolf huffed and he puffed and he puffed and he huffed — but he did not blow the house down.

'I will get up on to the roof. I will get in!' said the Big Bad Wolf. And he got up on to the roof.

The three little pigs got a big pot of boiling water.

The Big Bad Wolf was on the roof!

'I am coming down the chimney,' he shouted.

Then he fell, Plop! into the big pot of boiling water!

The three little pigs joined hands and sang *Who's afraid of the Big Bad Wolf! That is the end of the Big Bad Wolf!*

The three happy little pigs still live in their little house of bricks.

Who killed Cock Robin?

Who killed Cock Robin?
  I, said the Sparrow,
With my bow and arrow,
  I killed Cock Robin.

Who saw him die?
  I, said the Fly,
With my little eye,
  I saw him die.

Who caught his blood?
  I, said the Fish,
With my little dish,
  I caught his blood.

Who'll make his shroud?
  I, said the Beetle,
With my thread and needle,
  I'll make his shroud.

Who'll dig his grave?
  I, said the Owl,
With my spade and show'l,
  I'll dig his grave.

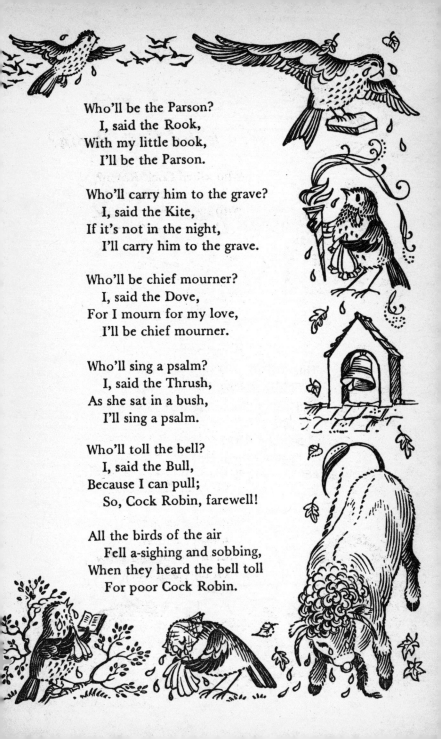

Who'll be the Parson?
   I, said the Rook,
With my little book,
   I'll be the Parson.

Who'll carry him to the grave?
   I, said the Kite,
If it's not in the night,
   I'll carry him to the grave.

Who'll be chief mourner?
   I, said the Dove,
For I mourn for my love,
   I'll be chief mourner.

Who'll sing a psalm?
   I, said the Thrush,
As she sat in a bush,
   I'll sing a psalm.

Who'll toll the bell?
   I, said the Bull,
Because I can pull;
   So, Cock Robin, farewell!

All the birds of the air
   Fell a-sighing and sobbing,
When they heard the bell toll
   For poor Cock Robin.

This is the house that Jack built.
  This is the MALT
That lay in the house that Jack built.

This is the RAT
  That ate the malt,
That lay in the house that Jack built.

THE HOUSE THAT JACK BUILT

This is the CAT,
   That killed the rat,
That ate the malt,
   That lay in the house that Jack built.

This is the DOG,
   That worried the cat,
That killed the rat,
   That ate the malt,
That lay in the house that Jack built.

This is the COW with the crumpled horn,
   That tossed the dog,
That worried the cat,
   That killed the rat,
That ate the malt,
   That lay in the house that Jack built.

This is the MAIDEN all forlorn,
   That milked the cow with the crumpled horn,
That tossed the dog,
   That worried the cat,
That killed the rat,
   That ate the malt,
That lay in the house that Jack built.

This is the MAN all tattered and torn,
  That kissed the maiden all forlorn,
That milked the cow with the crumpled horn,
  That tossed the dog, that worried the cat,
That killed the rat, that ate the malt,
  That lay in the house that Jack built.

This is the PRIEST all shaven and shorn,
  That married the man all tattered and torn,
That kissed the maiden all forlorn,
  That milked the cow with the crumpled horn,
That tossed the dog, that worried the cat,
  That killed the rat, that ate the malt,
That lay in the house that Jack built.

This is the COCK that crowed in the morn,
  That waked the priest all shaven and shorn,
That married the man all tattered and torn,
  That kissed the maiden all forlorn,
That milked the cow with the crumpled horn,
  That tossed the dog, that worried the cat,
That killed the rat, that ate the malt,
  That lay in the house that Jack built.

THE HOUSE THAT JACK BUILT

This is the FARMER who sowed the corn,
That kept the cock that crowed in the morn,
That waked the priest all shaven and shorn,
That married the man all tattered and torn,
That kissed the maiden all forlorn,
That milked the cow with the crumpled horn,
That tossed the dog, that worried the cat,
That killed the rat, that ate the malt,
That lay in the house that Jack built.

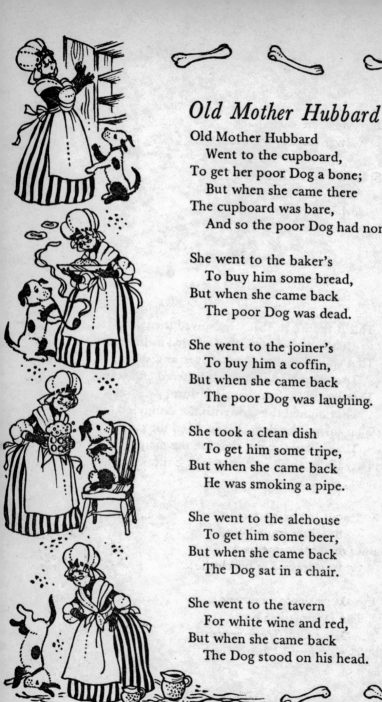

Old Mother Hubbard

Old Mother Hubbard
　　Went to the cupboard,
To get her poor Dog a bone;
　　But when she came there
The cupboard was bare,
　　And so the poor Dog had none.

She went to the baker's
　　To buy him some bread,
But when she came back
　　The poor Dog was dead.

She went to the joiner's
　　To buy him a coffin,
But when she came back
　　The poor Dog was laughing.

She took a clean dish
　　To get him some tripe,
But when she came back
　　He was smoking a pipe.

She went to the alehouse
　　To get him some beer,
But when she came back
　　The Dog sat in a chair.

She went to the tavern
　　For white wine and red,
But when she came back
　　The Dog stood on his head.

She went to the hatter's
   To buy him a hat,
But when she came back
   He was feeding the cat.

She went to the barber's
   To buy him a wig,
But when she came back
   He was dancing a jig.

She went to the fruiterer's
   To buy him some fruit,
But when she came back
   He was playing the flute.

She went to the cobbler's
   To buy him some shoes,
But when she came back
   He was reading the news.

She went to the sempstress
   To buy him some linen,
But when she came back
   The Dog was a-spinning.

She went to the hosier's
   To buy him some hose,
But when she came back
   He was dressed in his clothes.

The Dame made a curtsey,
   The Dog made a bow;
The Dame said, 'Your servant,'
   The Dog said, 'Bow wow.'

The Gingerbread Man

A little old lady
Once took a flat pan
And made for her husband
A Gingerbread Man.

The strange little man was made in this wise,
He had almonds for fingers, and currants for eyes;
He was dress'd in the brownest of brown little suits,
With little brown trousers and tiny brown boots.

As the man to her husband the old lady bore,
He suddenly jumped from the pan to the floor,
And scampered as fast as his little brown feet
Would carry him into the quaint little street.

The old lady's husband,
Who wanted a bite,
Ran out to prevent
Mr. Gingerbread's flight.

THE GINGERBREAD MAN

The good wife came after,
But quicker than she
Was a brisk little dog
Who was out for a spree.

The little brown man cared never a pin;
He ran past the dog, crying out with a grin
(While doggie barked loudly and on they all ran):
'You cannot catch me, I'm the Gingerbread Man!'

The little old lady ran well in the hunt;
And so did her husband, with doggie in front;
But the Gingerbread Man laughed aloud in his glee:
'Though you all may be clever, you cannot catch me!'

A big tabby cat
With a very fierce face
Saw Gingerbread coming
And took up the chase.

A sturdy policeman,
Slow pacing his beat,
Fell in with the others
And raced down the street.

The little brown man ran quicker and quicker;
The crowd at his heels grew thicker and thicker;
All shouted as loud as they could while they ran:
'Stop thief! He's a runaway Gingerbread Man!'

They chased him for many and many a mile,
But Gingerbread Man ran in wonderful style.
Sighed the policeman, 'I wonder if ever we can
Catch up with this fleet-footed Gingerbread Man.'

THE GINGERBREAD MAN

A dapper young soldier
Next took up the chase,
Though nothing he knew
Of the facts of the case.

Then a horse, with a neigh,
Bounded into the throng,
And with clattering hoofs
Galloped madly along.

Uphill and downhill the race did not pause,
For all were determined to stick to the cause;
With ease did the Gingerbread Man keep ahead,
But many behind him were very near dead.

They dashed into valleys; they raced over hills;
They splashed into cool little silvery rills;
They climbed over gates, and they leapt over stiles;
They ran and they shouted for hundreds of miles.

A gentle old cow,
By the noise frantic sent,
Rushed into the crowd,
Raising dust as she went.

And a cunning old crow
Left his favourite tree
To follow the chase
With the greatest of glee.

On through the country, and on through the towns;
On through the forests, and over the downs;
And when he looked back at the hurrying crowd
The little brown man felt exceedingly proud!

THE GINGERBREAD MAN

The dog and the cat, the horse and the cow,
The crow and the soldier, were all panting now;
The little old lady was weary indeed,
Although she kept on at a marvellous speed.

A sleepy-eyed owl
Woke and stared at the sight,
Then spreading his wings
Joined Jim Crow in the flight.

Some threshers at work
In a barnyard with flails
Took quick to their heel
And leapt over the rails.

But though the crowd grew, and increased as time went,
The little brown man seemed extremely content,
And laughed as he saw how they all ran and ran
And yet couldn't catch him — the Gingerbread Man.

He capered in frolic, he shouted with glee:
'For all you're so many, you cannot catch me!
Although you are running as fast as you can,
I'm faster, for I am the Gingerbread Man!'

Some mowers were mowing
A meadow hard by,
But couldn't resist
The hue and the cry.

What shrieking and shouting arose as they sped
In chase of the man made of sweet gingerbread!
Some fell on their faces, hard pushed from behind,
But picked themselves up, and not one seemed to mind.

THE GINGERBREAD MAN

The threshers, the mowers, the horse and the crow
Were all out of breath, but continued to go,
But the dog and the cat, although hot, did the best,
And ran, with their tongues out, in front of the rest.

In fact, with such zeal and such vigour they ran
They might have caught up with the Gingerbread Man;
When, all of a sudden, he turned to the right,
Scrambled over a wall, and was lost to their sight.

But there was a river
With rushes and rocks,
And high on the bank sat
A cunning old fox.

'Oh, where are you going, my Gingerbread Man?'
Asked the fox. 'I will help you along, if I can.
Although I'm a fox I can swim like a fish,
And will take you across on my back if you wish.'

The little brown man thanked the fox with a bow,
And said: 'If you're ready I'll go with you now.'
He jumped on his muzzle in less than a trice . . .
But foxes are cunning and ginger is nice,

And Gingerbread vanished
In less than a twink.
Now where did he go to? . . .
I leave you to think!

A Frog he would a-wooing go

A frog he would a-wooing go,
    Heigho, says Rowley,
Whether his mother would let him or no.
    With a rowley powley, gammon and spinach,
Heigho, says Anthony Rowley!

So off he set with his opera hat,
    Heigho, says Rowley,
And on the road he met with a rat.
    With a rowley powley, gammon and spinach,
Heigho, says Anthony Rowley!

'Pray Mr Rat, will you go with me,'
    Heigho, says Rowley,
'Kind Mrs Mousey for to see?'
    With a rowley powley, gammon and spinach,
Heigho, says Anthony Rowley!

When they came to the door of Mousey's hall,
    Heigho, says Rowley,
They gave a loud knock, and they gave a loud call.
    With a rowley powley, gammon and spinach,
Heigho, says Anthony Rowley!

A FROG HE WOULD A-WOOING GO

'Pray Mrs Mouse, are you within?'
   Heigho, says Rowley,
'Oh, yes, kind sirs, I'm sitting to spin.'
   With a rowley powley, gammon and spinach,
Heigho, says Anthony Rowley!

'Pray Mrs Mouse, will you give us some beer?'
   Heigho, says Rowley,
'For Froggy and I are fond of good cheer.'
   With a rowley powley, gammon and spinach,
Heigho, says Anthony Rowley!

'Pray Mr Frog, will you give us a song?
   Heigho, says Rowley,
But let it be something that's not very long.'
   With a rowley powley, gammon and spinach,
Heigho, says Anthony Rowley!

'Indeed, Mrs Mouse,' replied the Frog,
   Heigho, says Rowley,
'A cold has made me as hoarse as a hog.'
   With a rowley powley, gammon and spinach,
Heigho, says Anthony Rowley!

'Since you have caught cold, Mr Frog,' Mousey said,
   Heigho, says Rowley,
'I'll sing you a song that I have just made.'
   With a rowley powley, gammon and spinach,
Heigho, says Anthony Rowley!

But while they were all a merry-making,
   Heigho, says Rowley,
A cat and her kittens came tumbling in.
   With a rowley powley, gammon and spinach,
Heigho, says Anthony Rowley!

A FROG HE WOULD A-WOOING GO

The cat seized the rat by the crown,
   Heigho, says Rowley,
The kittens they pulled the little mouse down.
   With a rowley powley, gammon and spinach,
Heigho, says Anthony Rowley!

This put Mr Frog in a terrible fright,
   Heigho, says Rowley,
He took up his hat, and he wished them good-night.
   With a rowley powley, gammon and spinach,
Heigho, says Anthony Rowley!

But as Froggy was crossing over a brook,
   Heigho, says Rowley,
A lily-white duck came and gobbled him up.
   With a rowley powley, gammon and spinach,
Heigho, says Anthony Rowley!

So there was an end of one, two, and three,
   Heigho, says Rowley,
The Rat, the Mouse, and the little Frog-gee!
   With a rowley powley, gammon and spinach,
Heigho, says Anthony Rowley!

The Cock, the Mouse and the Little Red Hen

A cock, a mouse and a little red hen lived in a little house on the top of a hill. It was a sweet little house with a little green door, a little red roof and five little windows with little green shutters.

On another hill not very far away, stood another little house but this house was ugly. It had a broken down door, dirty windows and black shutters. In this house lived a family of bad foxes, bad Father Fox and three bad little foxes. The three little foxes said to Father Fox, 'Father, we are very hungry. Will you get us a big fat hen or a cock for our dinner?'

Father Fox was thinking, 'I see a little house on that hill. In that little house lives a cock, a mouse and a little red hen. I will take my sack and go and catch them for my little foxes.' So Father Fox set off with his sack on his back.

In the little house on the other hill the cock and the mouse were feeling very cross and kept on grumbling. The little red hen was not cross, and she was getting the breakfast.

'Who will go and fetch the sticks for the fire?' she said.

'Not I,' said the cock.

'Not I,' said the mouse.

'Then I will fetch them myself,' said the little red hen, and off she ran to get the sticks.

'Who will fill the kettle?' said the little red hen.

'Not I,' said the cock.

'Not I,' said the mouse.

'Then I will do it myself,' said the little red hen and off she went to fill the kettle.

'Who will help me get the breakfast?' said the little red hen.

'Not I,' said the cock.

'Not I,' said the mouse.

'Then I will do it myself,' said the little red hen and she hurried off to the kitchen to cook the breakfast.

At breakfast the cock and the mouse grumbled and grumbled. Then the cock upset the milk jug and the mouse grumbled more than ever.

After breakfast the little red hen said, 'Who will help me make the beds?'

'Not I,' said the cock.

'Not I,' said the mouse.

'Then I will do it myself,' said the little red hen and went up to make the beds.

The bad Father Fox crept up the hill and into the garden. He crept up to the little house and peeped in at the window. The cock and the mouse were fast asleep.

Bang! Bang! went the fox on the little green door.

The cock woke up. He jumped up and went to the door and in rushed the bad old fox.

'Cock a doodle do! Cock a doodle do!' yelled the cock, but the fox grabbed him and popped him into his sack. He then grabbed the little mouse and popped her into the sack with the cock.

The little red hen ran down to see what was the matter and bad Father Fox grabbed her and popped her into his sack with the cock and the mouse. Then he took a long string out of his pocket and wound it round the mouth of the sack and off he went down the hill with the sack on his back.

'I wish I had not been so cross,' said the cock.

'I wish I had not grumbled so much,' said the mouse.

'You must not be too sad,' said the little red hen, 'it is

never too late to mend. See, I have got my little bag and in it I have my little scissors, a needle and cotton and a thimble. You will soon see what I am going to do.'

The sun was very hot and the sack was very heavy. Bad Father Fox sat down under a tree to rest and soon he fell asleep.

The little red hen got out her little scissors and began to snip at the sack. Snip, snip, snip, went her little scissors. She cut a wee hole in the sack and the mouse scrambled out.

'Run and get a stone just as big as yourself,' said the little red hen. The mouse was soon back with a stone just as big as himself. 'Pop it into the sack,' said the little red hen. So the mouse popped the stone into the sack.

The little red hen snipped and snipped at the hole until it got bigger and bigger.

THE COCK, THE MOUSE and THE LITTLE RED HEN

Then out jumped the cock. 'Go and fetch a stone just as big as yourself,' said the little red hen. Soon the cock was back with a stone just as big as himself and he popped it into the sack. Then the little red hen hopped out. She soon found a stone just as big as herself and popped it into the sack.

Then with her needle and cotton she mended the hole in the sack. The cock, the mouse and the little red hen ran up the hill and into the little house.

Bang! The little red hen shut the door, the cock ran up to shut the windows and the mouse ran round and shut the little green shutters.

Bad Father Fox was still asleep under the tree. At last he woke up. 'It must be getting late,' he said, 'I must hurry home with the dinner for my little foxes,' and he picked up his sack and went stamp, stamp down the hill as far as the river. Splash! Splash! He began to cross the river but the stones in the sack were so heavy that he tripped and tumbled into the deep water and was drowned.

The cock and the mouse never grumbled after that. The cock got the sticks for the fire and the mouse filled the kettle and helped to sweep and dust the little house. No foxes were ever seen after that, and I think the cock, the mouse and the little red hen still live in the sweet little house with the little green door, a little red roof and five little windows with little green shutters.

Matilda

Who told Lies, and was Burned to Death.

A Cautionary Tale by Hilaire Belloc

Matilda told such Dreadful Lies,

It made one Gasp and Stretch one's Eyes;
Her Aunt, who, from her Earliest Youth,
Had kept a Strict Regard for Truth,

Attempted to Believe Matilda:
The effort very nearly killed her,
And would have done so, had not She
Discovered this Infirmity.
For once, towards the Close of Day,
Matilda, growing tired of play,

And finding she was left alone,
Went tiptoe

to

the Telephone
And summoned the Immediate Aid
Of London's Noble Fire-Brigade.
Within an hour the Gallant Band
Were pouring in on every hand,
From Putney, Hackney Downs and Bow,
With Courage high and Hearts a-glow
They galloped, roaring through the Town,

'Matilda's House is Burning Down!'
Inspired by British Cheers and Loud
Proceeding from the Frenzied Crowd,
They ran their ladders through a score
Of windows on the Ball Room Floor;
And took Peculiar Pains to Souse
The Pictures up and down the House,

Until Matilda's Aunt succeeded
In showing them they were not needed
And even then she had to pay
To get the Men to go away!

　　·　·　·　·　·　·

It happened that a few Weeks later
Her Aunt was off to the Theatre
To see that Interesting Play

MATILDA

The Second Mrs. Tanqueray.

She had refused to take her Niece
To hear this Entertaining Piece:
A Deprivation Just and Wise
To Punish her for Telling Lies.
That Night a Fire *did* break out—
You should have heard Matilda Shout!
You should have heard her Scream and Bawl,

And throw the window up and call
To People passing in the Street—
(The rapidly increasing Heat
Encouraging her to obtain
Their confidence)—but all in vain!
For every time She shouted 'Fire!'

They only answered 'Little Liar!'
And therefore when her Aunt returned,

Matilda, and the House, were Burned.

Some Nonsense Poetry
by D'Arcy Wentworth Thompson

1

There lived an old man in a garret,
    So afraid of a little tom-cat,
That he pulled himself up to the ceiling,
    And hung himself up on his hat.

And for fear of the wind and the rain
    He took his umbrella to bed —
I've half an idea that silly old man
    Was a little bit wrong in his head.

2

An inquisitive Cock Sparrow
 Asked every man in Wales,
Why Parrots had long noses,
 And foxes had long tails.

Some said that Foxes used their tails
 In winter for a muff;
And Parrots' noses were all long,
 Because they all took snuff.

But the reason, so it seems to me,
 As perhaps it will to you,
Is that they once tried short tails,
 And short tails wouldn't do.

3

Two little Dogs went out for a walk,
    And it was windy weather,
So for fear the wind should blow them away,
    They tied their tails together.

They tied their tails with a yard of tape,
    And the wind it blew and blew
As sharp and keen as a carving-knife,
    And cut the tape in two.

And away and away, like kites in the air
    Those two little Dogs flew about,
Till one little Dog was blown to bits.
    And the other turned inside out.

4

In London-town Dame Trottypeg
   Lived high up in a garret,
And with her lived a wee pet Dog,
   A Tom-cat, and a Parrot.

A cleverer or a funnier Dog
   I'm sure you never saw;
For, like a sailor, he could dance
   A hornpipe on one paw.

And all the while the Doggie danced,
   That Pussy-cat was able
Just like a flute to play his tail
   Upon the kitchen table.

But what a tongue, and O what brains
   Were in that Parrot's head!
It took two men to understand
   One half the things he said.

The Tale of the Turnip

Once upon a time there lived a little old man, a little old woman, a black and white cat and a wee grey mouse and they all lived together in a little house down under a hill. One day the little old man said to his wife, 'I am going into the garden to plant a seed.' 'A seed?' said his wife, 'what kind of a seed?' 'A turnip seed,' replied the little old man. So he took his spade and went to plant his turnip seed.

He dug a wee hole and he popped the seed in. 'There,' he said to himself, 'I have planted my seed. Now I must water it to make it grow into a fine big turnip.'

Each morning the little old man went out to water his turnip seed, and each day the sun shone down on the little seed and it began to grow.

It grew, and it grew, and it grew! It grew until it was as big as the old man's head — and still it grew! It grew, and it grew until it was twice as big as the old man's head! When it measured three times as much as the old man's head, the old man said to his wife, 'Today I am going to pull up the turnip. Put a big pot on the fire and get some water boiling and we will all have boiled turnip for dinner.'

The little old woman got a pot, the biggest pot she could find and she filled it with water and put it on the fire and the little old man went out into the garden to pull up the turnip. He took hold of the turnip and he pulled and he pulled — he pulled and he pulled and he pulled! but he could not pull up the turnip.

So the little old man called to the little old woman, 'Wife, wife! Come and help me pull up the turnip.'

The little old woman took hold of the little old man and

53

they pulled and they pulled, but they could not pull up the turnip. Then the little old woman called to the little girl, 'Little girl, little girl! Come and help us pull up the turnip.' So the little girl took hold of the little old woman and the little old woman took hold of the little old man and they pulled and they pulled and they pulled! — but they could not pull up the turnip.

So the little girl called to the black and white cat, 'Little cat, little cat! Will you come and help us pull up the turnip?' The black and white cat came running into the garden and the black and white cat took hold of the little girl, the little girl took hold of the little old woman and the little old woman took hold of the little old man — and they pulled and they pulled and they pulled! — but they could not pull up the turnip! Then the black and white cat called to the wee grey mouse, 'Wee grey mouse, wee grey mouse! Come and help us pull up the turnip.' The wee grey mouse came running out of the house and the wee grey mouse took hold of the black and white cat, the black and white cat took hold of the little girl, the little girl took hold of the little old woman and the little old woman took hold of the little old man — and they pulled and they pulled and they pulled and they pulled! — and at last up came the turnip!

The little old man fell on top of the little old woman, the little old woman fell on top of the little girl, the little girl fell on top of the black and white cat and the black and white cat fell on top of the wee grey mouse! — but they had pulled up the turnip!

They all got up and they took the turnip indoors. It was so heavy that they could hardly lift it and it measured three times as much as the old man's head!

When they got it indoors the little old woman cut it up and put it into the big pot of boiling water and they all had boiled turnip for dinner.

Limericks
by Edward Lear

There was an old lady of Chertsey,
   Who made a remarkable curtsey;
She twirled round and round
   Till she sank underground,
Which distressed all the people of Chertsey.

There was an Old Man with a beard,
   Who said: 'It is just as I feared! —
Two Owls and a Hen,
   Four Larks and a Wren,
Have all built their nests in my beard!'

There was an Old Man with a nose,
Who said: 'If you choose to suppose
That my nose is too long,
You are certainly wrong!'
That remarkable man with a nose.

There was a Young Lady whose chin
Resembled the point of a pin;
So she had it made sharp,
And purchased a harp,
And played several tunes with her chin.

There was an Old Person whose habits
   Induced him to feed upon rabbits;
When he'd eaten eighteen
   He turned perfectly green,
Upon which he relinquished those habits.

There was an Old Man of Peru,
   Who watched his wife making a stew:
But once by mistake,
   In a stove she did bake
That unfortunate Man of Peru.

There was a Young Lady whose nose
   Was so long it reached to her toes;
So she hired an old lady,
   Whose conduct was steady,
To carry that wonderful nose.

There was an Old Person of Rheims,
   Who was troubled with horrible dreams;
So, to keep him awake,
   They fed him on cake,
Which amused that Old Person of Rheims.

There was an Old Man of the South,
  Who had an immoderate mouth;
But in swallowing a dish,
  That was quite full of fish,
He was choked, that Old Man of the South.

There was an Old Person of Tring,
  Who embellished his nose with a ring;
He gazed at the moon
  Every evening in June,
That ecstatic Old Person of Tring.

There was an Old Man of Coblenz,
   The length of whose legs was immense;
He went with one prance
   From Turkey to France,
That surprising Old Man of Coblenz.

There was an Old Man of Leghorn,
   The smallest that ever was born;
But quickly snapped up he
   Was once by a puppy,
Who devoured that Old Man of Leghorn.

There was an Old Person of Gretna,
    Who rushed down the crater of Etna;
When they said 'Is it hot?'
    He replied: 'No, it's not!'
That mendacious Old Person of Gretna.

There was an Old Person of Spain,
    Who hated all trouble and pain;
So he sat on a chair,
    With his feet in the air,
That umbrageous Old Person of Spain.

There was an Old Man on whose nose,
  Most birds of the air could repose;
But they all flew away
  At the closing of day,
Which relieved that Old Man and his nose.

There was an Old Man of Aosta,
  Who possessed a large cow, but he lost her;
But they said: 'Don't you see
  She has rushed up a tree?
You invidious Old Man of Aosta!'

There was an Old Person of Rye,
  Who went up to town on a Fly;
But they said: 'If you cough,
  You are safe to fall off!
You abstemious Old Person of Rye!'

There was a Young Lady whose nose
  Continually prospers and grows;
When it grew out of sight,
  She exclaimed in a fright:
'Oh! Farewell to the end of my Nose!'

There was a Young Lady of Corsica,
  Who purchased a little brown Saucy-cur,
Which she fed upon Ham
  And hot Raspberry Jam,
That expensive Young Lady of Corsica.

There was a Young Person of Ayr,
  Whose Head was remarkably square:
On the top, in fine weather,
  She wore a Gold Feather,
Which dazzled the people of Ayr.

Four Poems from
The English Struwwelpeter

1. Augustus who would not eat any soup

Augustus was a chubby lad;
   Fat ruddy cheeks Augustus had;
And everybody saw with joy
   The plump and hearty healthy boy.
He ate and drank as he was told,
   And never let his soup get cold.
But one day, one cold winter's day,
   He scream'd out: 'Take the soup away!
O take the nasty soup away!
   I won't have any soup today.'

THE STORY OF AUGUSTUS

Next day, now look, the picture shows
  How lank and lean Augustus grows!
Yet, though he feels so weak and ill,
  The naughty fellow cries out still:
'Not any soup for me, I say:
  O take the nasty soup away!
I won't have any soup today.'

The third day comes; O what a sin
  To make himself so pale and thin!
Yet, when the soup is put on table,
  He screams, as loud as he is able:
'Not any soup for me, I say:
  O take the nasty soup away!
I won't have any soup today.'

Look at him, now the fourth day's come!
  He scarcely weighs a sugar-plum;
He's like a little bit of thread;
  And on the fifth day, he was — dead!

66

2. *Little Suck-a-Thumb*

One day, Mamma said: 'Conrad dear,
   I must go out and leave you here.
But mind now, Conrad, what I say,
   Don't suck your thumb while I'm away.
The great tall tailor always comes
   To little boys that suck their thumbs,
And ere they dream what he's about,
   He takes his great sharp scissors out
And cuts their thumbs clean off — and then,
   You know, they never grow again.'

THE STORY OF LITTLE SUCK-A-THUMB

Mamma had scarcely turn'd her back,
    The thumb was in, Alack! Alack!
The door flew open, in he ran,
    The great, long, red-legg'd scissor-man.
Oh! children, see! the tailor's come
    And caught out little Suck-a-Thumb.

Snip! snap! snip! the scissors go;
    And Conrad cries out: 'Oh! oh! oh!'
Snip! snap! snip! They go so fast,
    That both his thumbs are off at last.

Mamma comes home; there Conrad stands,
    And looks quite sad, and shows his hands —
'Ah!' said Mamma, 'I knew he'd come
    To naughty little Suck-a-Thumb.'

3. Fidgety Philip

'Let me see if Philip can
  Be a little gentleman;
Let me see if he is able
  To sit still for once at table.'
Thus Papa bade Phil behave;
  And Mamma look'd very grave.

But fidgety Phil,
  He won't sit still;
He wiggles
  And giggles,
And then, I declare,
  Swings backwards and forwards
And tilts up his chair,
  Just like any rocking-horse —

'Philip! I am getting cross!'
  See the naughty restless child
Growing still more rude and wild,
  Till his chair falls over quite.
Philip screams with all his might,
  Catches at the cloth, but then
That makes matters worse again.
  Down upon the ground they fall,
Glasses, plates, knives, forks and all.
  How Mamma did fret and frown,
When she saw them tumbling down!
  And Papa made such a face!
Philip is in sad disgrace.
  Where is Philip, where is he?

Fairly cover'd up, you see!
  Cloth and all are lying on him;
He has pull'd down all upon him.
  What a terrible to-do!
Dishes, glasses, snapt in two!
  Here a knife, and there a fork!
Philip, this is cruel work.
  Table all so bare, and ah!
Poor Papa and poor Mamma
  Look quite cross, and wonder how
They shall make their dinner now.

4. Johnny head-in-air

As he trudg'd along to school,
  It was always Johnny's rule
To be looking at the sky
  And the clouds that floated by;
But what just before him lay,
  In his way,
Johnny never thought about;
  So that everyone cried out:
'Look at little Johnny there,
  Little Johnny Head-in-Air!'

Running just in Johnny's way,
  Came a little dog one day;
Johnny's eyes were still astray
  Up on high,
In the sky;
  And he never heard them cry:
'Johnny, mind, the dog is nigh!'
  Bump!
  Dump!
Down they fell, with such a thump,
  Dog and Johnny in a lump!

THE STORY OF JOHNNY HEAD-IN-AIR

Once with head as high as ever,
   Johnny walk'd beside the river.
Johnny watch'd the swallows trying
   Which was cleverest at flying.
Oh! what fun!
   Johnny watch'd the bright round sun
Going in and coming out;
   This was all he thought about.
So he strode on, only think!
   To the river's very brink,
Where the bank was high and steep,
   And the water very deep;
And the fishes in a row,
   Stared to see him coming so.

One step more! Oh! sad to tell!
   Headlong in poor Johnny fell.
And the fishes, in dismay,
   Wagg'd their tails and ran away.
There lay Johnny on his face,
   With his nice red writing-case;
But, as they were passing by,
   Two strong men had heard him cry;
And, with sticks, these two strong men
   Hook'd poor Johnny out again.

Oh! you should have seen him shiver
   When they pull'd him from the river.
He was in a sorry plight!
   Dripping wet, and such a fright!
Wet all over, everywhere,
   Clothes, and arms, and face, and hair:
Johnny never will forget
   What it is to be so wet.

And the fishes, one, two, three,
   Are coming back again, you see;
Up they came the moment after,
   To enjoy the fun and laughter.
Each popp'd out his little head,
   And to tease poor Johnny, said:
'Silly little Johnny, look,
   You have lost your writing-book!'

The First Pike

On the night of Ivanov's Day (that is the day of Saint John, which is Midsummer) there was born the pike, a huge fish, with such teeth as never were. And when the pike was born the waters of the river foamed and raged, so that the ships in the river were all but swamped, and the pretty young girls who were playing on the banks ran away as fast as they could, frightened, they were, by the roaring of the waves, and the black wind and the white foam on the water. Terrible was the birth of the sharp-toothed pike.

And when the pike was born he did not grow up by months or by days, but by hours. Every day it was two inches longer than the day before. In a month it was two yards long; in two months it was twelve feet long; in three months it was raging up and down the river like a tempest, eating the bream and the perch, and all the small fish that came in its way. There was a bream or a perch swimming lazily in the stream. The pike saw it as it raged by, caught it in its great white mouth, and instantly the bream or the perch was gone, torn to pieces by the pike's teeth, and swallowed as you would swallow a sunflower seed. And bream and perch are big fish. It was worse for the little ones.

What was to be done? The bream and the perch put their heads together in a quiet pool. It was clear enough that the great pike would eat every one of them. So they called a meeting of all the little fish, and set to thinking what could be done by way of dealing with the great pike, which had such sharp teeth and was making so free with their lives.

They all came to the meeting — bream, and perch, and

roach, and dace, and gudgeon; yes, and the little ersh with his spiny back.

The silly roach said, 'Let us kill the pike.'

But the gudgeon looked at him with his great eyes, and asked, 'Have you got good teeth?'

'No' says the roach, 'I haven't any teeth.'

'You'd swallow the pike, I suppose?' says the perch.

'My mouth is too small.'

'Then do not use it to talk foolishness,' said the gudgeon; and the roach's fins blushed scarlet, and are red to this day.

'I will set my prickles on end,' says the perch, who has a row of sharp prickles in the fin on his back. 'The pike won't find them too comfortable in his throat.'

'Yes,' said the bream; 'but you will have to go into his throat to put them there, and he'll swallow you all the same. Besides, we have not all got prickles.'

There was a lot more foolishness talked. Even the minnows had something to say, until they were made to be quiet by the dace.

Now the little ersh had come to the meeting, with his spiny back, and his big front fins, and his head all shining in blue and gold and green. And when he had heard all they had to say, he began to talk.

'Think away,' says he, 'and break your heads, and spoil your brains, if ever you had any; but listen for a moment to what I have to say.'

And all the fish turned to listen to the ersh, who is the cleverest of all the little fish, because he has a big head and a small body.

'Listen,' says the ersh. 'It is clear enough that the pike lives in this big river, and that he does not give the little fish a chance, crunches them all with his sharp teeth, and swallows them ten at a time, I quite agree that it would be much better for everybody if he could be killed; but not one of us is strong enough for that. We are not strong enough to kill him; but we can starve him, and save ourselves at the same time. There's no living in the big river while he is here. Let all us little fish clear out, and go and live in the little rivers that flow into the big. There the waters are shallow, and we can hide among the weeds. No one will touch us there, and we can live and bring up our children in peace, and only be in danger when we go visiting from one little river to another. And as for the great pike, we will leave him alone in the big river to rage hungrily up and down. His teeth will soon grow blunt, for there will be nothing for him to eat.'

All the little fish waved their fins and danced in the water when they heard the wisdom of the ersh's speech. And the ersh and the roach, and the bream and the perch, and the dace and the gudgeon left the big river and swam up the little rivers between the green meadows. And there they began again to live in peace and bring up their little ones, though the cunning fishermen set nets in the little rivers and caught many of them on their way. From that time on there have never been many little fish in the big river.

And as for the monstrous pike, he swam up and down the great river, lashing the waters, and driving his nose through the waves, but found no food for his sharp teeth. He had to take to worms, and was caught in the end on a fisherman's hook. Yes, and the fisherman made a soup of him — the best fish soup that ever was made. He was a friend of mine when I was a boy, and he gave me a taste in my wooden spoon.

Arthur Ransome

RED RIDING HOOD

In a pretty cottage, not far from a wood, lived a forester, his wife, and their little girl.

Across the wood, in another cottage, lived the little girl's Grandmother.

She was very fond of her little granddaughter, and to keep her warm and cosy she made her a pretty red cloak and a hood to go with it.

Whenever the little girl went out she wore the red cloak and the hood. And so all the people called her Little Red Riding Hood.

One day when Little Red Riding Hood's mother was baking some cakes she was told that the Grandmother was ill in bed. So she took down a basket and filled it with dainties.

Among other things she put into it a home-made cake and a little pot of butter.

Then she called Little Red Riding Hood to her and said: 'Little Red Riding Hood, take this basket and go to your Grandmother and bring me word how she is.'

So Little Red Riding Hood set off across the wood, wearing her red cloak and her hood, and carrying on her arm the basket in which lay the home-made cake and the little pot of butter.

It was a beautiful day when Little Red Riding Hood set off. The sun was shining, the birds were singing, and all along the path were fresh, sweet flowers.

Every now and then Little Red Riding Hood stopped to pick a flower.

'They will make a nice posy for Grandmother,' she thought.

And so she went on picking flowers and quite forgot how quickly the time was going.

The wood across which Little Red Riding Hood had to go was very wide. There were many paths in it. The trees were high and their branches were thick.

But Little Red Riding Hood had been through it many times before, and so she went happily on her way, her flowers in her hand, and her basket on her arm, to see her poor old Grandmother.

Suddenly she met a Wolf. He looked at her red cloak and the basket on her arm, then he stopped and said to her politely:

'Tell me, little girl, what is your name?'

'I am called Little Red Riding Hood,' she answered, 'because of my cloak and my hood.'

'And where are you going, my dear?' said the Wolf.

'I am going to see my Grandmother,' said Little Red Riding Hood. 'She is ill in bed, and so Mother has sent me with this basket to take her a home-made cake and a little pot of butter.'

'Then where does your Grandmother live, my dear?' asked the Wolf.

'In a cottage by itself on the other side of the wood,' said Little Red Riding Hood.

'I see,' said the Wolf. 'Well, as she is ill in bed, perhaps I will come and visit her myself. You take this path, and I will take that one, and let us see who will get there first.'

So the Wolf took one path and Little Red Riding Hood took the other, and off they both went.

No sooner was the Wolf out of sight than he began to run across the forest as fast as ever he could.

'I must get to the cottage first,' he thought, ' and then I can eat up the Grandmother before Little Red Riding Hood gets there.' So off the wicked Wolf ran to the cottage where the poor old woman lived.

Meanwhile, Little Red Riding Hood went slowly on her way. She was very happy. She did not guess what the wicked Wolf meant to do.

Soon the Wolf came to the edge of the wood. He looked round him and soon he saw the little cottage standing all by itself. Within it lay the Grandmother, ill in bed.

The Wolf went up to the cottage and knocked softly on the door.

'Who is there?' the old woman called out.

'Little Red Riding Hood,' said the Wolf, in a voice just like the little girl's. 'I have brought you a basket with a home-made cake and a little pot of butter.'

'Then pull at the bobbin and lift up the latch,' said the Grandmother.

The Wolf pulled at the bobbin, the latch flew up, and the door opened. Then he rushed upon the bed where the poor old woman lay ill, and he swallowed her up before she could say a single word.

Then the wicked Wolf put on the poor old Grandmother's cap and her nightgown and jumped into the bed.

'When Little Red Riding Hood gets here,' he thought, 'she will think I am her Grandmother, and so I shall be able to eat her up too.'

So the wicked Wolf lay in the old woman's bed, waiting

for poor Little Red Riding Hood.

All this time Little Red Riding Hood had been walking through the wood. But she had stopped so often to pick flowers that at last she had quite lost her way. 'Oh dear!' she cried. 'I have lost the path! However shall I find the cottage where Grandmother lives!'

But just then she caught sight of a Woodman. He was busy at work, chopping up a great tree.

'He will tell me the way,' said Little Red Riding Hood, and so she ran up to him, saying: 'Woodman, I have lost my way. Please tell me where I am.'

The Woodman stopped chopping the tree and looked at Little Red Riding Hood.

'What is your name, little girl?' he said kindly.

'I am called Little Red Riding Hood,' she said, 'because of my cloak and my hood.'

'Then where are you going?' said the Woodman.

'I am going to see my Grandmother,' she answered. 'She is ill in bed, and so I am taking her a home-made cake and a little pot of butter.'

'And where does she live?' said the Woodman.

'In a cottage by itself on the other side of the wood,' said Little Red Riding Hood. 'But I have lost my way, and I do not know how to find it.'

'I will show you,' said the Woodman. 'I know the way quite well.'

So he showed Little Red Riding Hood where to go, and before very long she found she was quite close to the cottage.

Little Red Riding Hood went up to the cottage and knocked gently at the door.

'Who is there?' called out the Wolf, speaking just like her Grandmother.

'Little Red Riding Hood,' answered the child. 'I have

brought you a basket with a home-made cake and a little pot of butter.'

'Then pull at the bobbin and lift up the latch,' said the Wolf, in the Grandmother's voice.

So Little Red Riding Hood pulled at the bobbin and lifted the latch, and then she stepped inside the room.

She did not dream that harm could come to her in Grandmother's quiet cottage.

She had not heard of the Wolf's cruel nature, and he had seemed to be so kind.

'Put down the basket and come and lie down on the bed by me,' said the Wolf, pretending to be very ill.

So Little Red Riding Hood put the basket on the floor and then she went toward the bed.

'Oh, Grandmother!' she cried. 'What great ears you have got!'

'All the better to hear you with, my dear,' said the Wolf.

'But, Grandmother, what big eyes you have got!'

'All the better to see you with, my dear.'

'And, Grandmother, dear, what a great nose you have got!'

'All the better to smell you with, my dear,' said the cunning Wolf.

'But your mouth is so big, and your teeth are so sharp!'

'All the better to eat you with, my dear!' said the Wolf.

The poor child was now very frightened, and the Wolf saw that she had found out who he was.

So, without more ado, he sprang at poor Little Red Riding Hood, meaning to eat her up.

But Little Red Riding Hood flew across the room and out at the door.

As she ran she cried out with fright.

The Wolf was quickly at her heels, and it seemed that nothing could save her from his cruel jaws.

But the Woodman, who was still chopping the tree, heard her cries. Up he came, his sharp axe in his hand. The Wolf sprang toward him; the Woodman lifted his axe. He struck a fierce blow and the wicked Wolf lay dead.

Little Red Riding Hood got safely back to her parents after all.

How the Camel got its Hump

In the beginning of years, when the world was so new-and-all, and the Animals were just beginning to work for Man, there was a Camel, and he lived in the middle of a Howling Desert because he did not want to work; and besides, he was a Howler himself. So he ate sticks and thorns and tamarisks and milkweed and prickles, most 'scrutiating idle; and when anybody spoke to him he said 'Humph!' Just 'Humph!' and no more.

Presently the Horse came to him on Monday morning, with a saddle on his back and a bit in his mouth, and said, 'Camel, O Camel, come out and trot like the rest of us.'

'Humph!' said the Camel; and the Horse went away and told the Man.

Presently the Dog came to him, with a stick in his mouth, and said, 'Camel, O Camel, come and fetch and carry like the rest of us.'

'Humph!' said the Camel; and the Dog went away and told the Man.

Presently the Ox came to him, with the yoke on his neck, and said, 'Camel, O Camel, come and plough like the rest of us.'

'Humph!' said the Camel; and the Ox went away and told the Man.

At the end of the day the Man called the Horse and the Dog and the Ox together, and said, 'Three, O Three, I'm very sorry for you (with the world so new-and-all); but that Humph-thing in the Desert can't work, or he would have been here by now, so I am going to leave him alone, and you must work double-time to make up for it.'

HOW THE CAMEL GOT HIS HUMP

That made the Three very angry (with the world so new-and-all), and they held a palaver, and an *indaba*, and a *punchayet*, and a pow-wow on the edge of the Desert; and the Camel came chewing milkweed *most* 'scrutiating idle, and laughed at them. Then he said, 'Humph!' and went away again.

Presently there came along the Djinn in charge of All Deserts, rolling in a cloud of dust (Djinns always travel that way because it is Magic), and he stopped to palaver and pow-wow with the Three.

'Djinn of All Deserts,' said the Horse, '*is* it right for any one to be idle, with the world so new-and-all?'

'Certainly not,' said the Djinn.

'Well,' said the Horse, 'there's a thing in the middle of your Howling Desert (and he's a Howler himself) with a long neck and long legs, and he hasn't done a stroke of work since Monday morning. He won't trot.'

'Whew!' said the Djinn, whistling, 'that's my Camel, for all the gold in Arabia! What does he say about it?'

'He says "Humph!"' said the Dog; 'and he won't fetch and carry.'

'Does he say anything else?'

'Only "Humph!"; and he won't plough,' said the Ox.

'Very good,' said the Djinn. 'I'll humph him if you will kindly wait a minute.'

The Djinn rolled himself up in his dust-cloak, and took a bearing across the desert, and found the Camel most 'scruciatingly idle, looking at his own reflection in a pool of water.

'My long and bubbling friend,' said the Djinn, 'what's this I hear of your doing no work, with the world so new-and-all?'

'Humph!' said the Camel.

The Djinn sat down, with his chin in his hand, and began

HOW THE CAMEL GOT HIS HUMP

to think a Great Magic, while the Camel looked at his own reflection in the pool of water.

'You've given the Three extra work ever since Monday morning, all on account of your 'scruciating idleness,' said the Djinn; and he went on thinking Magics, with his chin in his hand.

'Humph!' said the Camel.

'I shouldn't say that again if I were you,' said the Djinn; 'you might say it once too often. Bubbles, I want you to work.'

And the Camel said 'Humph!' again; but no sooner had he said it than he saw his back, that he was so proud of, puffing up and puffing up into a great big lolloping humph.

'Do you see that?' said the Djinn. 'That's your very own humph that you've brought upon your very own self by not working. Today is Thursday, and you've done no work since Monday, when the work began. Now you are going to work.'

'How can I,' said the Camel, 'with this humph on my back?'

'That's made a-purpose,' said the Djinn, 'all because you missed those three days. You will be able to work now for three days without eating, because you can live on your humph; and don't you every say I never did anything for you. Come out of the Desert and go to the Three, and behave. Humph yourself!'

And the Camel humphed himself, humph and all, and went away to join the Three. And from that day to this the Camel always wears a humph (we call it 'hump' now, not to hurt his feelings); but he has never yet caught up with the three days that he missed at the beginning of the world, and he has never yet learned how to behave.

Rudyard Kipling

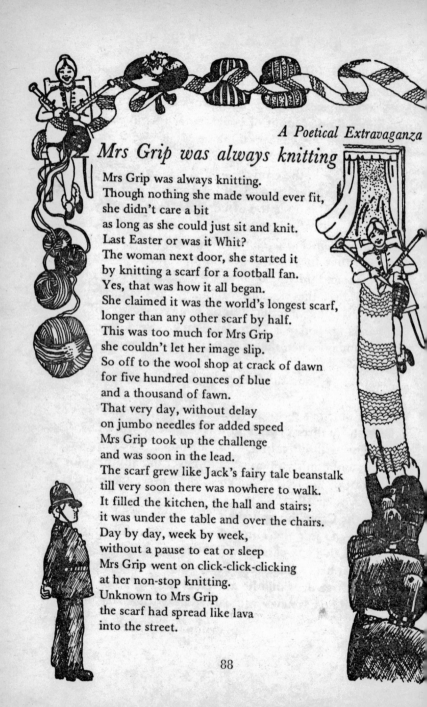

Mrs Grip was always knitting

Mrs Grip was always knitting.
Though nothing she made would ever fit,
she didn't care a bit
as long as she could just sit and knit.
Last Easter or was it Whit?
The woman next door, she started it
by knitting a scarf for a football fan.
Yes, that was how it all began.
She claimed it was the world's longest scarf,
longer than any other scarf by half.
This was too much for Mrs Grip
she couldn't let her image slip.
So off to the wool shop at crack of dawn
for five hundred ounces of blue
and a thousand of fawn.
That very day, without delay
on jumbo needles for added speed
Mrs Grip took up the challenge
and was soon in the lead.
The scarf grew like Jack's fairy tale beanstalk
till very soon there was nowhere to walk.
It filled the kitchen, the hall and stairs;
it was under the table and over the chairs.
Day by day, week by week,
without a pause to eat or sleep
Mrs Grip went on click-click-clicking
at her non-stop knitting.
Unknown to Mrs Grip
the scarf had spread like lava
into the street.

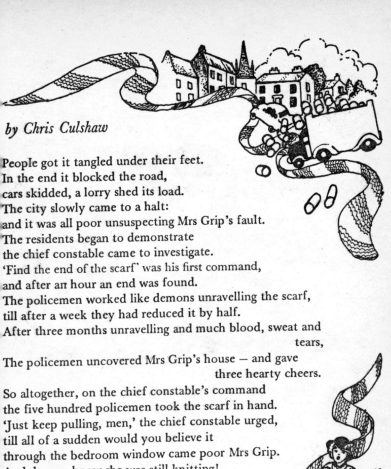

by Chris Culshaw

People got it tangled under their feet.
In the end it blocked the road,
cars skidded, a lorry shed its load.
The city slowly came to a halt:
and it was all poor unsuspecting Mrs Grip's fault.
The residents began to demonstrate
the chief constable came to investigate.
'Find the end of the scarf' was his first command,
and after an hour an end was found.
The policemen worked like demons unravelling the scarf,
till after a week they had reduced it by half.
After three months unravelling and much blood, sweat and
                                                 tears,
The policemen uncovered Mrs Grip's house — and gave
                                   three hearty cheers.

So altogether, on the chief constable's command
the five hundred policemen took the scarf in hand.
'Just keep pulling, men,' the chief constable urged,
till all of a sudden would you believe it
through the bedroom window came poor Mrs Grip.
And do you know she was still knitting!
There she was sitting,
safe and sound at the chief constable's feet.
The scarf had cushioned her fall.
She was a little dazed, but
she amazed them all, by turning
to the chief constable — him a six footer
and her a mere tich —
and saying, angrily:
'Now look what you've made me do —
                       I've dropped a stitch.'

THE PIED PIPER

The people of Hamelin had much to make them happy —
a pleasant town, with a deep green river running through
it, cosy gabled houses, flowering meadows, and plenty of
rosy-cheeked little boys and girls to go and pick the
flowers on fine days. But the people of Hamelin had also
something to make them very far from happy, and that
was the vast number of rats which insisted upon running
about everywhere. These rats were of all colours and sizes
that rats *can* be, black, white, brown, and grey; some no
bigger than mice and some as large as puppies. And they
did a tremendous amount of damage, for they nibbled and
munched everything they could reach, and the luckless
people of Hamelin could never think of a way to get rid of
these unwelcome guests. They tried putting down traps,
and they tried putting down poison; in vain! They tried
terriers, and they tried pussy-cats, and they tried praying

to the patron-saint of Hamelin, but *all* in vain!

Then one fine day the sound of a pipe was heard in the great open market-square before the main church, and the merchants who ran out to hear the music saw that the piper was a very queer-looking fellow indeed, long and lank, with a swarthy skin and mysterious, mocking green eyes. But the oddest thing about him was his dress, which was of two colours, scarlet and yellow, like the dress of some court fool.

As the people gathered round him, the piper stopped piping and began to sing,

> 'Who lives shall see
> That I am he,
> The man who can catch rats!'

When they heard the words of the song the people were much excited.

'Take him to the Mayor and the Town Council!' they cried all together. Now at that very moment the Mayor and the Town Council happened to be holding yet another meeting to discuss the plague of rats with which Hamelin was afflicted. The piper, followed by the chattering crowd, was brought before them.

'Are you a ratcatcher?' asked the Mayor.

'I am he who can catch rats,' returned the stranger.

'You have come to the right place, if you want a job,' said the Councillors.

'So I understand. And I am willing to clear your town of every rat that is in it before the sun sets to-night.'

'Sorcery, sorcery!' cried the crowd. 'He is a wizard — let us have nothing to do with him!'

'Peace!' said the Mayor, looking very serious. 'Leave it to the Mayor — leave it to me.'

'Leave it to the Mayor,' murmured all the Councillors.

'I am willing,' repeated the stranger, 'to clear Hamelin of

rats before sunset. But you must pay me a silver florin for every rat.'

'A silver florin for every rat,' cried the crowd. 'Why that would mean millions of florins! He is mad!'

'A florin a head,' said the piper. 'Those are my terms.'

'Done!' said the Mayor, finely. 'A bargain's a bargain. You shall receive a florin a head.'

'So be it. The deed will be done at moonrise. I advise the people of Hamelin to remain indoors while I am at work. But there is no reason why they should not look out of their windows. Till moonrise, good sirs!'

When the piper had retired to his room at the inn, the people of Hamelin began to discuss the Mayor's bargain with great energy. Some said that a florin a head would come to a terribly big sum of money. Some said the piper was an impostor. Others said that he was Satan himself. But the Councillors wagged their heads very wisely, and said, 'Leave it to the Mayor!'

At moonrise the piper appeared in the market-place again, and at the sound of his pipe the heads were thrust from every window for a mile round. At first he played slowly and softly, but soon the tune became swift and gay, the sort of tune that sets people tapping their heels and longing to dance. Then the people heard another sound beside the music of the pipe — a pattering, creaking, scampering sound, that grew louder and louder the longer the piper played. And from every house and cellar and barn, from every cupboard and garret and bin, a great army of rats came pouring into the market-place, all the rats of Hamelin.

The piper looked round, and saw that they were all there. Then, still piping, he set off toward the deep green river that runs through the town. The rats followed hard upon his heels.

On the brink of the river he paused, removed his pipe from his lips, and pointed to the middle of the flood, where the current ran strongest.

'In you go!' he said to the rats.

And in they went, one after another, by dozens, by scores, by hundreds. It was after midnight when the last rat of all reached the river's brink, and he was the first to pause before plunging in. A wise old rat he was, the largest of them all.

So the wise old rat leapt into the river, and vanished at the same spot where the rest of his tribe had gone down. The piper thereupon returned to his inn, and the townspeople to their beds.

There was peace in Hamelin that night — no crunching, no scuffling, no pattering, no creaking under the floor or behind the wainscot.

The next morning the Town Council met in the Town Hall, rejoicing loudly at the success of the pied piper. A few of the Councillors looked rather grave; they were thinking of the silver florins! But most of them believed in the wisdom of the Mayor, and you may be sure that he believed in it himself, most firmly. 'Trust me!' he said, whenever anyone seemed anxious.

The Council had not long been met together when the piper presented himself before them.

'The rats of Hamelin are gone,' declared he, 'I *could* tell you where, but I will *not* tell. It is enough for you to know that there were nine hundred and ninety nine thousand, nine hundred and ninety nine, and that not one of them will return. Now let us settle the score. You know our bargain.'

'Of course I do,' said the Mayor. 'A silver florin a head. By all means. Certainly. *But where are the heads?*'

'The heads!' repeated the piper, angrily. *'The heads!* If

94

you want them you can go and look for them. I have told
you how many there were. That is all that concerns you
and me now.'

'Dear me, no!' cried the Mayor, 'A bargain is a bargain,
Master Piper!'

And all the Councillors repeated after him, 'A bargain is a
bargain, you know!'

'You have broken *your* part of the agreement,' said the
Mayor, 'so, of course, you cannot hold us to *ours*. But we
do not wish to appear ungrateful. Here are fifty florins.'

'I will not take your fifty florins,' returned the piper, in
a stern voice, while his green eyes glinted fiercely. 'You
shall pay me yet — but not in money. Farewell, you wise
Councillors of Hamelin!'

'Ha, ha!' laughed the Councillors, 'what a foolish fellow!
We have got rid of our rats, and we have saved fifty florins!
Ha, ha!'

'I *told* you to leave it to me!' said the Mayor, puffing
with pride.

The next day was a Sunday, and all the townsfolk set
off for church. They did not take their children with them
to the first service of the day, but they looked forward to
being welcomed by their rosy-cheeked little boys and girls
on their return, and to eating their first Sunday dinner for
many years which had not been nibbled beforehand by
those wretched rats.

The service was over and all the fathers and mothers
went rustling home in their Sunday clothes, but their
houses seemed strangely dull and quiet. No little faces
peeping out of the windows, no little feet scampering down
the stairs, no little voices calling them to make haste, for it
was almost dinner time!

'Where are our children?'

Soon all the people were running to and fro, asking each

other that question, and hunting high and low, and calling the children by name to come forth from their hiding-places, for their joke had lasted long enough.

Presently some of the people who had gone to seek for the lost children in the meadows at the foot of a great hill on the outskirts of the town met a little lame boy, limping homeward on his crutches, and weeping bitterly. And from him they learned what had happened to the rest.

While all the grown-ups were at church, he said, the children heard the sound of the pied piper's pipe in the market-place, and ran out so that they might hear better. Never was such sweet music! Soon they all began to dance and sing, crowding round the piper, and clinging to his scarlet and yellow sleeves. When he began to march toward the meadows at the foot of the great hill, they all followed him, skipping and jumping, and keeping time to the merry airs he played. But when he reached those meadows, he did not stop. He went straight toward the mountain, and all the children followed. And when he reached the mountain he did not stop. He went straight on, and the mountain opened, and he walked into the mountain, and all the children followed. All, that is to say, except the little cripple. He could not run as fast as the others, and by the time he reached the mountain, the gap had closed again.

On hearing these things the people of Hamelin seized crowbars and sticks and hurried to the mountain in the hope that they might find some crack or seam, and open it up, and so find the piper and the children. Foremost among them was the Mayor, who had lost three dear little daughters and two handsome little sons. Poor man, never was he heard to say again, 'Leave it to the Mayor!' For the children did not come back. And where they went nobody can say, for they were never seen again.

Some Nonsense Poems by
Lewis Carroll

1. You are old, Father William

'You are old, Father William,' the young man said,
  'And your hair has become very white;
And yet you incessantly stand on your head —
  Do you think, at your age, it is right?'

'In my youth,' Father William replied to his son,
  'I feared it might injure the brain;
But, now that I'm perfectly sure I have none,
  Why, I do it again and again.'

'You are old,' said the youth, 'as I mentioned before.
  And have grown most uncommonly fat;
Yet you turned a back-somersault in at the door —
  Pray, what is the reason for that?'

'In my youth,' said the sage, as he shook his grey locks,
  'I kept all my limbs very supple
By the use of this ointment — one shilling the box —
  Allow me to sell you a couple?'

'You are old,' said the youth, 'and your jaws are too weak
  For anything tougher than suet;
Yet you finished the goose, with the bones and the beak —
  Pray, how did you manage to do it?'

'In my youth,' said his father, 'I took to the law,
  And argued each case with my wife;
And the muscular strength, which it gave to my jaw
  Has lasted the rest of my life.'

'You are old,' said the youth, 'one would hardly suppose
 That your eye was as steady as ever;
Yet you balanced an eel on the end of your nose —
 What made you so awfully clever?'

'I have answered three questions, and that is enough,'
 Said his father. 'Don't give yourself airs!
Do you think I can listen all day to such stuff?
 Be off, or I'll kick you down-stairs!'

2. *The Walrus and the Carpenter*

The sun was shining on the sea,
 Shining with all his might:
He did his very best to make
 The billows smooth and bright —
And this was odd, because it was
 The middle of the night.

The moon was shining sulkily,
 Because she thought the sun
Had got no business to be there
 After the day was done —
'It's very rude of him,' she said,
 'To come and spoil the fun!'

The sea was wet as wet could be,
 The sands were dry as dry.
You could not see a cloud because
 No cloud was in the sky:
No birds were flying overhead —
 There were no birds to fly.

The Walrus and the Carpenter
   Were walking close at hand:
They wept like anything to see
   Such quantities of sand:
'If this were only cleared away,'
   They said, 'it *would* be grand!'

'If seven maids with seven mops
   Swept it for half a year,
Do you suppose,' the Walrus said,
   'That they could get it clear?'
'I doubt it,' said the Carpenter,
   And shed a bitter tear.

'O Oysters, come and walk with us!'
   The Walrus did beseech.
'A pleasant walk, a pleasant talk,
   Along the briny beach:
We cannot do with more than four,
   To give a hand to each.'

THE WALRUS AND THE CARPENTER

The eldest Oyster looked at him,
But never a word he said:
The eldest Oyster winked his eye,
And shook his heavy head —
Meaning to say he did not choose
To leave the oyster-bed.

But four young Oysters hurried up,
All eager for the treat:
Their coats were brushed, their faces washed,
Their shoes were clean and neat —
And this was odd, because, you know,
They hadn't any feet.

Four other Oysters followed them,
And yet another four:
And thick and fast they came at last,
And more, and more, and more —
All hopping through the frothy waves,
And scrambling to the shore.

THE WALRUS AND THE CARPENTER

The Walrus and the Carpenter
  Walked on a mile or so,
And then they rested on a rock
  Conveniently low:
And all the little Oysters stood
  And waited in a row.

'The time has come,' the Walrus said,
  'To talk of many things:
Of shoes — and ships — and sealing wax —
  Of cabbages — and kings —
And why the sea is boiling hot —
  And whether pigs have wings.'

'But wait a bit,' the Oysters cried,
  'Before we have our chat;
For some of us are out of breath,
  And all of us are fat!'
'No hurry!' said the Carpenter.
  They thanked him much for that.

'A loaf of bread,' the Walrus said,
  'Is what we chiefly need:
Pepper and vinegar besides
  Are very good indeed —
Now, if you're ready, Oysters dear,
  We can begin to feed.'

'But not on us!' the Oysters cried,
  Turning a little blue.
'After such kindness, that would be
  A dismal thing to do!'
'The night is fine,' the Walrus said.
  'Do you admire the view?

'It was so kind of you to come!
   And you are very nice!'
The Carpenter said nothing but
   'Cut us another slice.
I wish you were not quite so deaf —
   I've had to ask you twice!'

'It seems a shame,' the Walrus said,
   'To play them such a trick.
After we've brought them out so far,
   And made them trot so quick!'
The Carpenter said nothing but,
   'The butter's spread too thick!'

'I weep for you,' the Walrus said:
   'I deeply sympathize.'
With sobs and tears he sorted out
   Those of the largest size,
Holding his pocket-handkerchief
   Before his streaming eyes.

'O Oysters,' said the Carpenter,
  'You've had a pleasant run!
Shall we be trotting home again?'
  But answer came there none —
And this was scarcely odd, because
  They'd eaten every one.

3. *Beautiful Soup*

Beautiful Soup, so rich and green,
  Waiting in a hot tureen!
Who for such dainties would not stoop?
  Soup of the evening, beautiful Soup!
  Soup of the evening, beautiful Soup!
    Beau—ootiful Soo—oop!
    Beau—ootiful Soo—oop!
Soo—oop of the e—e—evening,
  Beautiful, beautiful Soup!

Beautiful Soup! Who cares for fish,
  Game, or any other dish?
Who would not give all else for two p
  ennyworth only of beautiful Soup?
  Pennyworth only of beautiful soup?
    Beau—ootiful Soo—oop!
    Beau—ootiful Soo—oop!
Soo—oop of the e—e—evening,
  Beautiful, beauti—FUL SOUP!

The Wolf and the Fox

A foolish fox once made friends with a wolf. With his silky brush and pointed noise he fancied himself a fine smart fellow, and hardly knew at first which way to look he was so vain of his new company. But he soon found out that his new friend was not in love with him for his own sweet sake only, and that *being* a wolf, a wolf he *was*. For one thing, he was a greedy glutton and could never eat enough; and next, he had no manners.

'And what's for supper to-night?' he would say, his white teeth glinting in the moon. 'Bones! Bones! Again! Lor', friend Fox, if you can't get me anything really worth eating, I shall soon have to eat *you*.' This was an old joke now; and though he grinned as he said it, his sharp fangs and bloodshot eyes looked none too pleasant.

As for the fox he smiled on one side of his face but not on the other. 'Well, friend Wolf,' he said, 'keep up your spirits. There's a farmyard over the hill where some plump young lambs are fattening. Softly now, and away we go!'

So off they went together. When they reached the farmyard the fox sneaked in through the gate, snatched up one of the lambs, leapt over the stone wall and carried it off to the wolf. After which, he trotted round to the henhouse to get his own supper in peace. But when the wolf had finished off his lamb — leaving not so much as a bone for his friend to pick — he felt hungrier than ever, and determined to slip away himself and get the other.

But he was so clumsy in scrabbling over the stone wall of the farmyard that the old mother sheep heard him, and began bleating aloud in the darkness. At this the farmer, who was sitting in his kitchen, ran out with his dog and cudgel, and managed to give the wolf such a drubbing as he climbed back over the wall, that he came creeping back to the fox as wild with pain as he was with rage.

'A nice thing *you've* done,' he said to the fox. 'I went to fetch another lamb, and I'm beaten to a jelly.'

'Well,' said the fox, 'one's one and two's two; but enough is as good as a feast;' and he thought of the tasty

young pullet he had stolen for his own supper.

Next day they decided to be getting off into country where they were less well-known. After a pleasant afternoon's journey, they found themselves on the edge of a small green coppice basking in the sun. The wolf stretched himself out and soon fell asleep. He woke up as surly as a bear with a sore head.

'Come, rouse, friend Fox! Supper!' he bawled. 'What's for supper? No more lamb to-night. I'd sooner eat *you*!'

The fox trembled with rage, but he answered him civilly

and said: 'I seem to smell pancakes — rich pancakes. Squat here awhile, friend Wolf, and I'll see what I can do.'

He slipped off and away to the other side of the wood, and came to a house from whose brick chimneys a faint smoke was wreathing up into the evening air laden with so sweet and savoury an odour of pancakes that the fox lifted his nose into the air and snuffed and snuffed again. Then first he crept this way; and then he crept that way; and at last he stole in through an open window, and so into the pantry, and leaping up on to a shelf, carried off at least six of the pancakes.

The wolf swallowed them down without so much as a thank'ee, and champed for more. The glutton then asked the fox which way he had gone. The fox told him.

'You'll know the house by the smoke,' he said, 'and the window is by the water-butt. But step quiet, my friend, if go you must, for I heard voices.' The greedy wolf, thinking that if the fox came with him to the house he would expect a share of the pancakes that were left, at once scuffled off alone into the night to finish the dish.

But he made such a hullabaloo in the pantry as he went sprawling along the shelf, upsetting a great cooking crock as he did so, that the farmer and his wife, and the friends who had been supping with them, heard the noise and came rushing in, and gave him such a basting that he hardly escaped with his life.

When he had licked his bruises and got some breath into his body again, he came snarling back to the fox, and blamed *him* for his beating. The fox coughed and turned his head aside; he could hardly speak for rage and contempt. However, the duck he himself had supped off was still sweet in memory; so he answered the wolf smoothly, reminding him that he had been given a fair warning. 'Besides,' said he, 'as I've said before, enough is as good as a feast, friend Wolf; and with *some* sauces, much better.'

Yet, even now, the wolf had not learned his lesson. For, a very few evenings afterwards, though he could only limp along on three legs, and every bone in his body ached, he turned sullenly on his friend the fox, and said: 'Friend Fox, I'm sick and tired of you. You've no more wits than a rabbit. 'Sly,' indeed! Now see here; if before that moon up there has climbed an inch in the sky you don't get me a meat meal, a tasty meal, and plenty of it — a supper worth a gentleman's eating, I'm saying — then it will surely be the last of you, for I'm *done* with your shilly-shallying.'

The fox trembled and said, 'Softly, softly, friend Wolf; why lose your temper? I do my best. This very morning I heard that the human that lives by the stream on the other side of the hill yonder has been killing a pig. A fat pig — a very fat pig; a pig *stuffed* with fatness. And the salt pork of that pig is packed in a barrel in the human's cellar. Ah, I see your mouth watering. Come, we will go together.'

'Why, yes,' said the wolf, 'and you shall keep watch while I eat.'

So the fox led him off by a green ride through the woods and over the crest of the hill, and by a cart-track, till at last they came down to a mill. It was a clear moonlight night, with a sparkle of frost in the air. And as it chanced, there was a small, round-topped outside little door under the wall of the house that led into the cellar. The fox pushed up its latch; paused; sniffed; listened; sniffed again.

His green eyes glistened like fireballs, as he turned his sharp muzzle and looked back at the wolf. 'Follow,' he said, ' and do not so much as grin or gruff. The human of this house has a gun.'

The wolf, being overfed and overfat, only just managed to scramble through the doorway. But at last he followed the fox into the cellar, and was soon guzzling away at the barrel of salted pork.

'Tell me, friend Fox,' he said, glancing over his shoulder, his jaws dripping, 'why do you keep sniffing and snuffing about like that? Restrain yourself. It vexes me, it annoys me. How can I feed in comfort with you fidgeting and fretting? Keep still; and you shall, perhaps, have a gobbet or two for yourself by and by. All depends on what I leave!'

'Gobble on, gobble on,' said the fox meekly. 'There's plenty of time for me. But I warn you: don't make a noise, and don't eat too hearty!'

'Ah,' said the wolf, 'you thought this fat luscious feast of pork was for you, did you? And after all my pains in finding it! Have no fear, greedy-guts, there won't be much left when *I've* finished with it.'

At this, with a stroke of his paw and a heave of his shoulder, he turned the great salty tub clean over on the stones of the cellar; and a fine clatter it made.

Indeed, the miller, who was at that moment shaving himself in a looking-glass, hearing this noise in his cellar, supposed for a moment there was an earthquake. Then he snatched up his blunderbuss, and with the soapsuds still foaming on his cheek, came clumping down the steep stone steps into the cellar.

At first sound and whiff of him the fox was out through the hole at a bound, and in a moment or two his friend the wolf, stricken with terror, was struggling hard to follow him. But the greedy guzzler had so puffed and swilled himself out with his feast of pork that, wriggle and wrench as he might, he could not squeeze through the hole. So there he stuck. And the miller, although he had lost a good half of his pickled pork, at least gained a thick warm wolf's skin in exchange.

Meanwhile, the fox on the crest of the hill, hearing the roar of the blunderbuss, shivered a little, then danced a little dance all to himself in the moonlight. There and then he made up his mind that his next friend should be neither wolf nor glutton, but of his own size and liking; and one with a brush.

Walter de la Mare

Three Nonsense Poems
by Edward Lear

1. The Pobble who has no toes

The Pobble who has no toes
   Had once as many as we;
When they said 'Some day you may lose them all' —
   He replied: 'Fish fiddle de-dee!'
And his Aunt Jobiska made him drink,
   Lavender water tinged with pink,
For she said: 'The world in general knows
   There's nothing so good for a Pobble's toes!'

The Pobble who has no toes,
   Swam across the Bristol Channel;
But before he set out he wrapped his nose
   In a piece of scarlet flannel.
For his Aunt Jobiska said: 'No harm
   Can come to his toes if his nose is warm;
And it's perfectly known that a Pobble's toes
   Are safe — provided he minds his nose.'

THE POBBLE WHO HAS NO TOES

The Pobble swam fast and well,
    And when boats or ships came near him.
He tinkledy-binkledy-winkled a bell,
    So that all the world could hear him.
And all the Sailors and Admirals cried,
    When they saw him nearing the farther side —
'He has gone to fish, for his Aunt Jobiska's
    Runcible Cat with crimson whiskers!'

But before he touched the shore,
    The shore of the Bristol Channel,
A sea-green Porpoise carried away
    His wrapper of scarlet flannel.
And when he came to observe his feet,
    Formerly garnished with toes so neat,
His face at once became forlorn
    On perceiving that all his toes were gone!

And nobody ever knew
    From that dark day to the present,
Whoso had taken the Pobble's toes,
    In a manner so far from pleasant.
Whether the shrimps or crawfish gray,
    Or crafty Mermaids stole them away —
Nobody knew; and nobody knows
    How the Pobble was robbed of his twice five toes!

The Pobble who has no toes
    Was placed in a friendly Bark,
And they rowed him back, and carried him up,
    To his Aunt Jobiska's Park.
And she made him a feast at his earnest wish
    Of eggs and buttercups fried with fish —
And she said: 'It's a fact the whole world knows,
    That Pobbles are happier without their toes.'

2. *The Quangle-wangle's hat*

On the top of the Crumpetty Tree
 The Quangle-Wangle sat.
But his face you could not see,
 On account of his Beaver Hat.
For his Hat was a hundred and two feet wide,
 With ribbons and bibbons on every side
And bells, and buttons, and loops, and lace,
 So that nobody ever could see the face
Of the Quangle-Wangle Quee.

The Quangle-Wangle said
 To himself on the Crumpetty Tree:
'Jam; and jelly; and bread;
 Are the best of food for me!
But the longer I live on this Crumpetty Tree,
 The plainer than ever it seems to me
That very few people come this way,
 And that life on the whole is far from gay!'
Said the Quangle-Wangle Quee.

THE QUANGLE-WANGLE'S HAT

But there came to the Crumpetty Tree,
    Mr and Mrs Canary;
And they said: 'Did ever you see
    Any spots so charmingly airy?
May we build a nest on your lovely Hat?
    Mr Quangle-Wangle, grant us that!
O please let us come and build a nest
    Of whatever material suits you best,
Mr Quangle-Wangle Quee!'

And besides, to the Crumpetty Tree
    Came the Stork, the Duck, and the Owl;
The Snail and the Bumble-Bee,
    The Frog, and the Fimble Fowl;
(The Fimble Fowl, with a Corkscrew leg);
    And all of them said: 'We humble beg,
We may build our homes on your lovely Hat —
    Mr Quangle-Wangle, grant us that!
Mr Quangle-Wangle Quee!'

And the Golden Grouse came there,
    And the Pobble who has no toes,
And the small Olympian bear,
    And the Dong with a luminous nose.
And the Blue Baboon, who played the flute,
    And the Orient Calf from the Land of Tute,
And the Attery Squash, and the Bisky Bat,
    All came and built on the lovely Hat
Of the Quangle-Wangle Quee.

And the Quangle-Wangle said
   To himself on the Crumpetty Tree:
'When all these creatures move
   What a wonderful noise there'll be!'
And at night by the light of the Mulberry moon
   They danced to the Flute of the Blue Baboon,
On the broad green leaves of the Crumpetty Tree,
   And all were as happy as happy could be,
With the Quangle-Wangle Quee.

3. *The Owl and the Pussy-cat*

The Owl and the Pussy-Cat went to sea
   In a beautiful pea-green boat,
They took some honey, and plenty of money,
   Wrapped up in a five-pound note.
The Owl looked up to the stars above,
   And sang to a small guitar,
'O lovely Pussy! O Pussy, my love,
   What a beautiful Pussy you are,
      You are,
      You are!
What a beautiful Pussy you are!'

THE OWL AND THE PUSSY-CAT

Pussy said to the Owl, 'You elegant fowl!
  How charmingly sweet you sing!
O let us be married! too long we have tarried,
  But what shall we do for a ring?'
They sailed away for a year and a day,
  To the land where the Bong-tree grows,
And there in a wood a Piggy-wig stood,
  With a ring at the end of his nose,
    His nose,
    His nose,
  With a ring at the end of his nose.

'Dear Pig, are you willing to sell for one shilling
  Your ring?' Said the Piggy, 'I will.'
So they took it away, and were married next day
  By the Turkey who lives on the hill.
They dined on mince, and slices of quince,
  Which they ate with a runcible spoon;
And hand in hand, on the edge of the sand,
  They danced by the light of the moon,
    The moon,
    The moon,
They danced by the light of the moon.

Teddy Robinson and
the Lord Mayor's Show

Teddy Robinson was a nice, big, comfortable, friendly teddy bear. He had light brown fur and kind brown eyes, and he belonged to a little girl called Deborah.

One day Teddy Robinson and Deborah were going to London to stay with Auntie Sue. Teddy Robinson was very excited.

'Don't forget to brush my fur specially well, will you?' he said. 'And are you *sure* my old trousers will do? And did you remember to pack my best purple dress?'

'Yes, of course,' said Deborah. 'But you've asked me all those questions three times already. I've got my own packing to do. Why are you making such a fuss?'

Teddy Robinson looked surprised. 'It isn't every teddy bear who has the chance of going to London,' he said. 'This is an Important Day for me. I must look my best.'

"Did you remember to pack my best purple dress?"

117

'All right,' said Deborah, 'but it's important for me too. As long as you're clean and neat you'll do very nicely. Now be a good boy and don't worry me till I've finished packing.'

So Teddy Robinson sat by the open door of the toy cupboard, and talked to the dolls who had all been put away inside.

'I'm sorry we shan't be able to take you as well,' he said, 'but I think it might be a little too much for you. (Anyway you weren't invited). You see, London is a big and important place, full of big and important people. But we'll tell you all about it when we get back.'

Then he gave them a kindly smile all round, and began singing to himself in a low, carefree growl,

> 'Hooray, hooray, hooray,
> I'm going to London today.
> An important bear,
> looking clean and neat,
> will soon be driving up the street.
> So wave a flag and shout "Hooray,"
> Teddy R's in town today.'

'But we haven't got a flag,' said the dolls.

'No, not you,' said Teddy Robinson. 'I was thinking about all the people in London.'

'Oh,' said the dolls. 'And will you wave a flag too?'

'Oh no,' said Teddy Robinson. 'You can't wave a flag at yourself. You might hit your own nose. I shall just look friendly and dignified. That's what important people do when people wave flags at them.'

'Oh,' said the dolls. 'Thank you for telling us.'

'It's a pleasure,' said Teddy Robinson. And he went on telling them about going to London until, one by one, they had all fallen asleep.

'Some people just don't know when anything's exciting,'

said Teddy Robinson.

'Well — no, poor things, but they're only little,' said Deborah, having a last look round the toy cupboard. 'I'm glad they're asleep.' And she shut the door on them.

Then it was time to go.

As they drove into London in Auntie Sue's car, Teddy Robinson got more and more excited. He bounced up and down on Deborah's lap, and stared at the huge buildings, and the crowds walking in the streets, and thought he had never seen so many people in his life.

'I bet they'd be surprised if they knew *I* was here,' he said to himself. 'I'm even surprised myself — and I *knew* I was coming.' And he began singing a little song to celebrate his arrival,

'Look who's come to London town —
fat and furry, big and brown —
look who's driving in that car.
Bless my boots, it's Teddy R!'

When they got held up in a traffic jam he was pleased to notice that several people smiled at him through the window. A big red bus drew up alongside and some children sitting inside stared down at him and pointed him out to their mother. She smiled too, and one little boy waved a flag at him.

As they drove on, he saw that the crowds on the pavement were growing thicker, and that all the children were holding flags or paper streamers.

'How nice of them to turn out to welcome us,' he said. But Deborah didn't hear, because she and Auntie Sue were busy talking about the Lord Mayor's Show. Teddy Robinson didn't interrupt, but sat up proudly, and tried to look clean and neat, and dignified and friendly all at the same time.

Then he heard Auntie Sue say, 'How lucky it should be today! I'd quite forgotten. We must find somewhere to park the car.' And before he had time to find out what was happening, they had driven up a side street, got out of the car, and were all running as fast as they could.

'What's happening?' said Teddy Robinson, puffing because Deborah was running so fast it made him out of breath.

'We're going to see the Lord Mayor's Show,' she said. 'Isn't it exciting? The Lord Mayor of London is driving along the Strand in a goiden coach, and if we're quick we shall see him.'

They turned into a road called Ludgate Hill. There were crowds of people on the pavement.

'Hold on to me,' said Auntie Sue.

Then they heard a noise of music and drums coming up the street. All the people shouted, 'Here they come!' and there was the sound of soldiers' marching feet. Everyone began pushing and jostling, and the smaller children in the crowd began wailing, 'I can't see-ee-ee! I can't see-ee-e!' and hitting people's legs with the flags they were trying to wave. Teddy Robinson couldn't see anything either, except one button on Deborah's coat.

Then a tall man, standing beside Auntie Sue, said, 'Shall I lift your little girl up?'

Teddy Robinson was just going to say, 'She isn't her little girl. She's mine,' when Auntie Sue said, 'Oh, yes please!' And she took Teddy Robinson from Deborah and tucked him under her own arm. Then Deborah was lifted up, high over their heads, on to the tall man's shoulder. She had a fine view. Teddy Robinson couldn't see quite so well, but he managed to squint through a gap between two people. The band played louder, and he began grunting happily to himself in time to the music.

Suddenly there was a big cheer, and the Lord Mayor of London came riding by in his golden coach.

TEDDY ROBINSON AND THE LORD MAYOR'S SHOW

The Lord Mayor was wearing a large three-cornered hat, made of curly black feathers, and a crimson robe trimmed with fur. Round his neck hung a heavy gold chain. Teddy Robinson could see him leaning out of the coach window, smiling, and waving his hand.

Everyone cheered and waved their flags, and Teddy Robinson thought he had never seen anyone quite so splendid before. 'That is a really remarkable hat,' he said to himself. And he wondered if he could ask for one like it for Christmas.

Behind the coach came a long procession of decorated cars and lorries, and people in fancy dress, but Teddy Robinson hardly saw them.

He had a picture in his mind of driving through London in a golden coach, wearing that remarkable hat, and waving a gracious paw to the crowds.

'I shall be the Lord Bear of London,' he said to himself, and began making up a little song under his breath,

> 'The Lord Bear of London
> is driving down the Strand,
> a homely bear with a friendly air,
> the best bear in the land.
> His name is Teddy Robinson — '

and then he got stuck, because he couldn't find a word to rhyme with his own name.

He was so busy trying to think of the next line, that he didn't even notice when the procession came to an end.

The tall man put Deborah down, and she said 'Thank you.' Auntie Sue leaned forward to straighten her coat, and said, 'Wasn't that fun?' And Teddy Robinson (quite by mistake, because he wasn't thinking what he was doing) slipped out from under her elbow and fell into the gutter.

Deborah and Auntie Sue walked away, still talking. Most of the other people walked away too. And Teddy Robinson

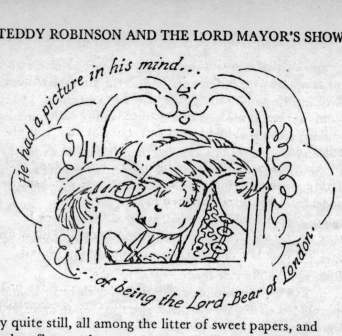

He had a picture in his mind... ...of being the Lord Bear of London.

lay quite still, all among the litter of sweet papers, and broken flags, and paper streamers, still thinking about being Lord Bear of London, and trying to find a word to rhyme with his own name.

The road was nearly empty now, and some pigeons flew down and began pecking in the gutter. One of them came waddling along towards him. It was very fat, and walked with its toes turned in.

'Coo!' said the pigeon. 'What can you be thinking of, lying there in all that rubbish?'

'I was thinking of being Lord Bear of London,' said Teddy Robinson, and tried to look as if he was lying there on purpose.

'Coo!' said the pigeon. 'Who are you, then? Are you someone important?'

'Yes, I'm Teddy Robinson. You may have heard of me.'

The pigeon looked interested. 'I know most of the important people in the City,' it said, 'but can't quite place you for the moment.'

It came nearer and stared harder.

'These are only my old trousers,' said Teddy Robinson. 'They didn't have time to make me any more. But, of course, I shan't wear *them* when I'm Lord Bear.'

The pigeon waddled round and stared at him from the other end.

'And I know my fur's getting a little thin on top,' said Teddy Robinson. 'But that won't matter. It won't show under my large three-cornered hat.'

The pigeon looked puzzled. It stood first on one leg, then on the other. Then it said rather quickly, 'This is the first I've heard of it. I must go and consult my friends.' And it waddled away to join the other pigeons.

They were pecking at a lump of popcorn someone had dropped in the gutter. Teddy Robinson could hear them talking together in low voices.

'He says he's going to be Lord Mayor of London.' 'Who?' 'That bear down there.' 'Coo! Do you know him?' 'No, do you?' 'Who can he be?' 'Coo, I wish I knew!'

Soon they all came strutting solemnly down the road and stood round Teddy Robinson in a ring.

'You don't by any chance belong to the Royal Family, do you?' said one of them.

'Oh, no,' said Teddy Robinson. 'I have a very nice family of my own.'

'Do you know the Queen?' said another.

'Oh, yes!' said Teddy Robinson.

'Have you been to Buckingham Palace?' they asked.

'Not yet. I'm going tomorrow,' said Teddy Robinson. He remembered Auntie Sue had promised to take them there.

'Did the Queen invite you?' they said.

'No,' said Teddy Robinson. 'She doesn't know I'm here yet. I hope it'll be a nice surprise for her.'

The pigeons moved away a little and put their heads together.

'Coo! Coo! Can it be true?' they said. 'Who can he be?' Then one of them said, 'I don't believe a word of it. He's making it up. Let's ask him something else.'

'Yes, do,' they all said. 'No, you.' 'Go on, do!' 'Coo! Coo! Coo!'

Then they all came back again.

'Have we ever seen you on the television?' they said.

'No, I don't think so,' said Teddy Robinson. 'I do sit on top sometimes when Deborah's looking in, but I don't think you could have seen me. I've never been right in the picture.'

The pigeons looked more puzzled than ever.

'What makes you think you're important, then?' they said.

'Being here, of course,' said Teddy Robinson. 'It isn't every teddy bear who has the chance of coming to London.'

'Coo, that's nothing!' said the pigeons. 'We live here. The City belongs to us. Who asked you to be Lord Mayor?'

'Nobody *asked* me,' said Teddy Robinson. 'I was only thinking it might be rather fun.'

'Well!' said the pigeons. 'We've been wasting all this time talking to somebody who's nobody! We pigeons are important people.' And they marched away angrily.

'Dear me,' said Teddy Robinson, feeling not quite so important himself. 'I wonder what made them so cross?'

Just then a small brown sparrow flew down and perched beside him on the kerb.

'Hullo-ullo! Waiting for Joe?' it chirped.

'Who's Joe?' asked Teddy Robinson.

'Who's Joe? What-ho! You don't know Joe? Well, bless my beak, I thought everyone knew Joe!' said the sparrow, and it burst into song,

'Joe, Joe,
Jolly old Joe!

He's the Most Important Person in the Lord Mayor's
Show!'

Then it flew up on to a high building.

'Well, fancy that,' said Teddy Robinson. 'I thought the
Lord Mayor's Show was over.' And he lay on his back,
wondering who Joe was, and when he was coming.

'It's funny,' he said to himself, 'the people thought the
Lord Mayor was important, and the pigeons thought *they*
were important. But nobody seems to think I am important
at all. What a silly old bear I am! I don't believe I'm anyone
special after all.'

There was a rumble of wheels behind him, and the sparrow
flew down again, chirping excitedly,

'What-ho!

Here comes Joe!

He'll clean up all the rubbish from the Lord Mayor's
Show!'

Teddy Robinson saw a man coming along, pushing a
small barrow, with a dustbin fitted into it. He was
sweeping the gutter as he went, and putting all the litter
into the bins. The sparrow watched him, chirping loudly.

'What cheer, my little cock-sparrow!' said the man. 'You
waiting for me, are you?' And he pulled a piece of cake
from his pocket and threw some crumbs to the sparrow.
The he saw Teddy Robinson.

'Hullo-ullo-ullo! What are *you* doing here?' he said. And
before Teddy Robinson had time to explain, Joe had picked
him up, dusted his fur, and sat him on top of the barrow.

'The gutter's no place for a chap like you,' he said,
winking at Teddy Robinson. Then he started pushing the
barrow up Ludgate Hill.

That sparrow was right, thought Teddy Robinson. Joe is
a very nice man.

He sat up straight (not too proud, and not too humble)

and began to enjoy the ride. 'I may not be anyone important,' he said to himself, 'but this is an excellent way of seeing London. It's so handy not having any windows. I can see all the way round without having to put my head out. I should have thought a little open-air coach like this might have been more handy for the Lord Mayor. It only wants painting gold.'

And smiling happily, he began making up a little song all about the Lord Bear of London, riding up the Strand, in an elegant open dust-cart, pulled along by hand.

. . . an elegant open dust-cart pulled along by hand.

The he saw the pigeons again. This time they were all lined up on an office building, high above the street.

'Coo!' they said, nudging each other and peering over the ledge. 'It looks as if he *is* somebody after all!'

Teddy Robinson looked up and gave them a gracious smile as he passed underneath.

And then, just as they reached St Paul's Cathedral, who should he see but Deborah and Auntie Sue! They were coming down the steps, and when they saw Teddy Robinson riding on top of the little dust-cart, they looked even more surprised than the pigeons.

'That's *Teddy Robinson!*' they both said together.

Deborah turned to look under Auntie Sue's arm, and Auntie Sue turned to look under Deborah's arm.

'I thought you were carrying him!' said Deborah.

'I thought *you* were!' said Auntie Sue. Then they both ran down to meet him.

Auntie Sue said 'Thank you' to Joe a great many times over, and Deborah hugged Teddy Robinson and told him how glad she was to see him.

'It is a pity you weren't with us,' she said, as they walked back to the car. 'We've just been in the biggest church in London.'

'It is a pity you weren't with me,' said Teddy Robinson. 'I've just been with the most important person in the Lord Mayor's Show.'

'But you can't have been,' said Deborah. 'The Lord Mayor went by ages ago.'

'The *important* person is the man who cleans the street afterwards,' said Teddy Robinson.

Deborah laughed, but Auntie Sue said, 'You know, that's rather clever of Teddy Robinson. The man who cleans the street *is* a very important person. I wonder how he knew.'

'A little bird told me,' said Teddy Robinson.

Much later on, when they were both tucked up in bed, Deborah said, 'Dear Teddy Robinson, I am glad I didn't lose you. I wouldn't change you for fifty Lord Mayors.'

'Nor would I,' said Teddy Robinson. 'I've been thinking, would it be a good idea if I had a label tied to my braces while I'm in London? Then if I get lost again, I shall know who I am.'

Deborah thought that was a very good idea. 'What shall

we put on it?' she said.

'I thought something quite plain and simple, like *TEDDY ROBINSON OF LONDON*,' he said. 'After all, it isn't as if I'm anyone important.'

'But of *course* you're important,' said Deborah. 'To me you're the Most Important Teddy Bear in the Whole World.'

And that is the end of the story about Teddy Robinson and the Lord Mayor's Show.

Joan G Robinson

The Story of Cruel Frederick

Here is cruel Frederick, see!
   A horrid wicked boy was he;
He caught the flies, poor little things,
   And then tore off their tiny wings,
He kill'd the birds, and broke the chairs,
   And threw the kitten down the stairs,
And oh! far worse than all beside,
   He whipp'd poor Mary, till she cried.

The trough was full, and faithful Tray
   Came out to drink one sultry day;
He wagg'd his tail, and wet his lip,
   When cruel Fred snatch'd up a whip,
And whipp'd poor Tray till he was sore,
   And kick'd and whipp'd him more and more.
At this, good Tray grew very red,
   And growl'd and bit him till he bled;

THE STORY OF CRUEL FREDERICK

Then you should only have been by,
To see how Fred did scream and cry!

So Frederick had to go to bed;
His leg was very sore and red!

The Doctor came and shook his head
And made a very great to-do,
And gave him nasty physic too.
But good dog Tray is happy now;

He has no time to say 'Bow-wow!'
He seats himself in Frederick's chair
And laughs to see the nice things there;
The soup he swallows, sup by sup —
And eats the pies and puddings up.

HANSEL AND GRETEL

Once upon a time there lived a poor woodcutter who had a boy and a girl called Hansel and Gretel. Their mother had died when they were quite tiny children, and after a time their father married a second wife who was not at all kind to her stepson and stepdaughter. The woodcutter, although he worked very hard, could not earn enough money to feed the whole family, and there were often empty plates on the table and hungry faces round it.

One night, when he and his wife thought that Hansel and Gretel were fast asleep, they began to say to each other that very soon there would be nothing to give the children.

'There is only one thing to be done,' said the cruel stepmother. 'Early tomorrow morning we will give each child a piece of bread, and then we will lead them into the very heart of the deep forest and leave them there. They will never be able to find their way home again.'

'My poor children!' cried the woodcutter, 'what will happen to them? I cannot leave them alone in the forest, to be eaten by wild beasts.'

'There is nothing else to be done,' returned the stepmother, firmly.

Now Hansel and Gretel were not asleep, and when they heard what their stepmother said, Gretel wept bitterly.

'Hush,' whispered Hansel. 'Don't be afraid. I have a plan.'

Presently, when the woodcutter and his wife were snoring, the boy crept out of his little wooden bed, unbarred the door of the hut, and tiptoed out into the moonlight. The grass outside was sprinkled with pure white pebbles that shone like drops of silver. Hansel filled his pockets with these pebbles and then went softly back to his sister.

'Sleep in peace, Gretel,' he said, 'God will not forsake us.'

Early next morning the stepmother came to wake the children.

'Up you lazy creatures,' she said. 'Your father is going to the forest to chop wood, and you are going with him. Here is a piece of bread for your dinner. Mind you don't lose it, for you will get no more.'

Hansel and Gretel made ready to go with their father. Gretel carried the bread in her apron, for Hansel's pockets were full of pebbles.

When the whole family had gone a little way toward the forest Hansel paused and looked back; presently he did this again; and when he did it for the third time, his father asked why he kept lagging behind. 'I can see our white cat sitting on the roof of the hut,' answered Hansel. 'It is bidding us Good-bye.'

'Nonsense,' said the stepmother, 'that is the sun shining on the white chimney.'

Hansel knew that quite well; but every time he looked back he had dropped a pebble from his pocket on the path.

When they had reached the inmost depths of the forest the father told the children to gather some fallen branches and dry twigs, so that he might make a fire. When the fire was lit, and crackling merrily, the stepmother said, 'Now, you two children can sit by the flame and eat your dinner. Your father is going to cut wood nearby, and I am going with him.'

Hansel and Gretel were a little bit frightened, but the sound of their father's axe cheered them, for while they heard it they knew he could not be far away. They grew drowsy soon, with the warmth of the fire, and at last they fell asleep. So early had they risen, and so far had they trudged, they both slept soundly till after the sun had set. Then they woke up with a start. Gretel began to cry.

'Hush, little sister,' said Hansel, 'the moon is rising. Look — there are my white pebbles. We can soon find our way home now.'

They set off hand-in-hand, and at daybreak they arrived at their father's hut, stiff and foot-sore, and their hair drenched with dew. When their stepmother saw them she tried to hide her anger as best she could.

'Wicked ones,' she exclaimed, 'why have you slept so long? Your father and I thought we should never see you again.'

The woodcutter, however, rejoiced greatly, for he had begun to regret that he had followed his wife's advice.

It was not long before she returned to the plan that had failed, and made up her mind to try again.

'Those children of yours,' she said one night, 'they eat the shelf bare, and yet they are always crying and saying they are hungry. There is only one thing to be done.'

'I will not do it,' returned the woodcutter, who knew quite well what she meant.

'We will do it tomorrow morning,' said the stepmother, firmly.

The children heard what was said, but this time Gretel did not cry. She was sure that Hansel would think of a plan even when he found he could get no more pebbles from the hut, which had been locked by the stepmother.

'Do not be afraid, little sister,' he said, 'the Good God will not forsake us. I shall think of another plan.'

At dawn the next day the stepmother came and woke them, and gave them a piece of bread. This time it was Hansel who took charge of it, and he broke it into small crumbs inside his pocket. When they had gone a few paces he paused and looked back, and then again, a little farther on. The third time he did this, his father asked him why he lagged behind.

'I am looking at our dove,' said Hansel. 'She is nodding us Good-bye.'

'Nonsense,' cried the stepmother, 'that is the sun shining on the white chimney.'

But Hansel managed to drop a crumb from time to time.

When they reached the very depths of the forest they were told to gather sticks as before. And when the fire was lit, the stepmother said, 'Sit here till we come back for you — we shall not be gone for long.'

Hansel had strewn all his bread along the path, but Gretel had kept a small piece, and this she shared with him. Presently they fell fast asleep, and when they awoke the forest was dark, and the moon had not yet risen. Gretel began to weep, but Hansel said, 'Wait till moon-rise. Then we shall be able to see the crumbs that I scattered.'

When the moon's silver globe began to shine beyond the fir-trees the children hastened to look for the crumbs. But not a single crumb could they find. The birds had eaten every one.

For three days Hansel and Gretel wandered through the forest. They had nothing but wild berries to eat, and at night they slept upon the red pine-needles under the trees. At last, just when they were beginning to lose heart altogether, they saw and heard a lovely little silver-coloured bird which hopped from branch to branch and sang sweetly. It was so pretty, and its song was so sweet, the children followed it, and presently, to their surprise they came to a little house. They had never seen a house like it before, and they thought it much more beautiful than if it had been built of silver and gold. For the walls were made of fine white bread and thick plum cake, the windows were of clear yellow toffee, and the roof was of gingerbread.

'What a nice house!' said Gretel.

'I am going to find out what this house tastes like!' cried Hansel. He stood on tip-toe and broke a piece off the roof while Gretel pulled a pane out of the window. They were eating happily when the door of the house opened, and a very old woman came tottering out, propped on a pair of crutches. Hansel and Gretel were so frightened that they dropped their cake and toffee on the ground. But the old woman did not seem at all cross.

'Come here, children,' she said. 'My eyes are none of the best — but you are very welcome.'

She passed her hand over their faces once or twice, and muttered to herself, 'They are thin now — far too thin — but we can soon alter that.' Then she said aloud, 'Come in, my dears, come in — I am very fond of children.'

Hansel and Gretel thought they had never met anyone so kind, and they wished they had had a stepmother like that. They followed her into the house, which was larger inside than they had expected, and there they saw a table spread for supper, and two little beds with bright-coloured counterpanes.

'Poor children,' said the old woman, 'I am sure you are still hungry.'

Hansel and Gretel were nearly always hungry. They explained to her that their father was very poor, too poor to give them enough to eat.

'You shall have pancakes for supper,' promised their

new friend. Never in their wildest dreams had Hansel and
Gretel imagined that there could be such good things to eat
as they had for supper that night. When they were fast
asleep in the two little beds the old woman came and felt
their thin cheeks again.

'Too thin,' she muttered, 'but we can soon alter that. I
will take the boy first.'

Now this old woman, who seemed so kind, was really a
witch, and when she said that she was fond of children, she
meant that she was fond of them for breakfast and dinner.
Like all witches, she had wicked red eyes that could not
see very far, and a great big nose with which she could
smell a human being a mile away. Her gingerbread-and-
toffee house was simply a trap in which to catch children,
and as she had not caught any for some time she was
delighted to see Hansel and Gretel.

When Hansel opened his eyes next morning he found
himself in a sort of wicker cage, and wondered what had
happened to him. Gretel was still asleep in her little bed
with the bright counterpane, but just as Hansel was going
to call to her to come and set him free, the old witch came
hobbling in.

'Wake up, child,' said the old witch. 'You must go to the
well and draw some water. I want to cook something nice
for your brother's breakfast.'

'Am I to have no breakfast?' asked Gretel.

'Not such a big breakfast as *his*,' returned the witch, 'I
want to make him nice and fat.'

'Why?' asked Gretel.

'So that he may taste good when I eat him for my
supper,' returned the old witch.

Poor Gretel burst into tears at the idea of Hansel
providing a supper for this terrible old witch, and Hansel
himself felt very much inclined to cry. 'I must think of a
plan,' said Hansel.

For four long weeks the witch kept Hansel in the wicker cage, plying him with all sorts of delicious food. Every morning she would say, 'Boy, stretch out your finger — I want to feel if you are getting fat!' and every morning Hansel would stretch out a piece of bone which he had found in the cage. The witch was so blind, she could not see that it was not his finger, and she wondered why he was so slow in getting fat, and how many more weeks she would have to wait for that supper to which she was looking forward so greedily.

At last she became impatient.

'Gretel,' she said, one morning, 'I will wait no longer. Hansel must be cooked today. You must help me to make the oven hot. He is to be baked in a pie.'

'Aren't you going to knead the dough first?' asked Gretel, trying to gain time.

'I have kneaded it already,' returned the witch.

Shedding bitter tears, poor Gretel brought the wood to kindle the fire under the oven. Soon it was crackling and blazing.

'I think the oven must be hot enough now,' said the witch, 'put your head in, Gretel, and tell me.'

Gretel put her head in, and, though it was really quite warm inside the oven, she said, 'It is still cold — you could never bake a pie in such a cold oven.'

'Add some more logs to the fire,' commanded the witch.

The logs spluttered and flamed, and the oven grew fearfully hot.

'Put your head in again, Gretel,' said the witch.

This time Gretel only pretended. She knew the witch was too blind to see what she was doing very well.

'It is not hot yet,' declared Gretel.

'You are tricking me,' cried the witch, 'I will find out the truth for myself!'

So she opened the oven-door, and peered inside, and Gretel gave her a sudden sharp push so that she fell head-over-heels.

Then Gretel shut the oven-door upon her, and drew the bolts. And inside the oven there was a big bang.

Meanwhile the little girl had run to the cage where Hansel was still a prisoner, and when she unbarred the wicker door her brother hopped out like a bird set free. They kissed each other with tears of joy, and danced about the witch's house singing at the top of their voices, for they were sure she could not hurt them any more.

Presently there was another big bang, and the oven split open, and there in the middle stood a huge gingerbread cake in the form of an old woman. The children gazed at it in wonder.

'I should not like to eat any of that gingerbread,' said Hansel.

'No,' agreed Gretel, 'neither should I. But let us take some of the toffee window-panes home with us, and a piece of the plum-cake wall.'

They began to explore the little house, and they found that all the drawers and cupboards were full of gold and silver coins. Hansel filled his cap and his pockets, and Gretel filled her apron, until they could carry no more.

'Now let us go home,' said Gretel.

They walked all day through the forest, and toward sunset they saw the smoke rising from the chimney of their father's hut. Then, tired though they were, they broke into a run. As they ran, the gold and silver coins came tumbling out on the grass.

The woodcutter was standing very sadly by the door of the hut, looking toward the forest where he had last seen his children. The cruel stepmother had died during the time that Hansel and Gretel were in the witch's house, and

he was quite alone. When he saw the little boy and girl
coming toward him he could hardly believe his eyes. So
happy were they all at this undreamt-of end to their
troubles, it was some time before they thought about
gathering up and counting the money from the witch's
hoard. There was enough of it to keep them all in comfort
for the rest of their lives.

SLEEPING BEAUTY

The goldsmiths in the service of a certain King were once delighted to receive an order from his Majesty for seven golden dishes, seven golden cups, seven golden forks, and seven golden spoons.

'The baby Princess is to be christened next week,' the Lord High Chamberlain explained to the goldsmiths, 'and these golden dishes and cups are for the seven fairy godmothers who are coming to the christening.'

When the Lord High Chamberlain had walked proudly away, the oldest of the King's goldsmiths said, 'In *my* young days *eight* fairy-godmothers were *always* invited to *every* royal christening.'

'To be sure they were,' agreed the second oldest, 'but the eighth one has gone to foreign parts — some say she has gone to the North Pole, and some say she has gone to the South. Anyway, nobody knows *where* she is. So, of course, the King and Queen couldn't invite her.'

'*Hum!*' said the third oldest goldsmith, 'that's a pity!'

The day fixed for the christening came, and the seven godmothers arrived at the palace, two in winged chariots, two on Arab steeds, two on camels and one upon an elephant. They gathered round the ivory cradle of the baby Princess and promised her all sorts of delightful things. One said that she would be the most beatiful Princess in the whole world, another that she would be the sweetest-tempered, another that she would be the cleverest, another that she would sing like a lark, another that she would dance like a blossom on the wind, another that everyone would love her, and another that she would never lack gold.

The King and Queen were delighted, and the whole company had sat down to the christening feast in the very best of tempers, when suddenly there was a sound of scratching and scraping in the courtyard of the palace, and the Lord High Chamberlain came running with a very white face to announce that a dragon had just alighted there, with yet *another* fairy guest.

The King and Queen hastened to welcome this unexpected fairy who was an uncommonly cross-looking old lady. They led her to a chair at the head of the table, and begged her to honour them by eating some of the christening-cake and the other good things spread out there, but most unfortunately they could only offer her a plate, cup, fork, and spoon of silver, as the golden ones had all been given to the seven other fairies.

The eighth fairy was most annoyed.

'You had forgotten me,' she said, in a gruff voice, 'but I will give you good cause to remember me hereafter. My sisters have promised many fair gifts to your daughter. *My* promise is that she will prick her finger on a spindle and die of the prick!'

At these cruel words everyone, including the seven godmothers, uttered a loud cry of horror. The Queen burst into tears. The King tore handfuls out of his beard. The

Lord High Chamberlain sobbed aloud. Then the youngest and kindest of the seven godmothers stepped forward and said, 'Do not be afraid, good people. Though I have not the power to undo what my sister has done, and though the Princess *must* prick her finger as has been foretold, I can alter her fate this much — that she will *not* die of the prick.'

At these words, the Queen wiped her eyes, the King ceased to tear his beard, and the Lord High Chamberlain stopped short in the middle of a sob.

'Wait,' said the fairy, 'I have not finished yet. When the Princess pricks her finger she will fall asleep — and she will not wake up again till the most perfect Prince in the world finds her, and kisses her on the cheek.'

When the fairies had departed, the eighth one growling and scowling to the last moment, the first thing that the King did was to summon his Parliament and make a new law that from that day no one should spin in his dominions, and that all spinning-wheels and spindles were to be chopped in small pieces and either burned or thrown into the sea. Sixteen years passed, and the hum of the spinning-wheel was never heard in the land. The Princess grew up beautiful and clever and good, just as her godmothers had promised, and everybody, even the crossest and hardest-hearted people, loved her.

One fine day, when her father was out hunting, and her mother and all the maids-of-honour were gathering cherries to make into tarts, the Princess thought she would like to explore some of the more ancient parts of the palace, which was a vast, rambling building more than a thousand years old. She went from room to room, and from tower to tower, climbing up narrow, twisting staircases, and getting her pretty slippers very dusty and cobwebby on the way. At last she came to a little door at the very top of a high, grim-looking tower, and from behind the door came a low humming sound such as she had never heard before.

Full of curiosity, the Princess opened the door, and saw an aged, wrinkled woman working with a wheel. So old was she, and so deaf, that nobody had thought of telling her about the law forbidding people to spin, and for sixteen years hers had been the only spinning-wheel in the land.

'What are you doing, good woman?' asked the Princess.

'I am spinning, my pretty young lady.'

'Is it very difficult to spin?'

'Not for such as have clear eyes and willing fingers.'

'Will you not show me how it is done?'

'Gladly, my pretty one. 'Tis many a long year now since I saw a young face in this old tower.'

The Princess sat down beside the old woman, eager to learn. But in her eagerness she seized the spindle by the sharp end, and the point pricked her finger. Only one tiny drip of blood appeared, but the poor Princess slipped from her chair on to the floor, and lay there as if she were dead.

The old woman, in great terror, ran to fetch help, and when the Princess had been carried down the twisting stairs and laid upon her own golden bed, the King and Queen saw the drop of blood on her finger and knew that the cruel fairy's promise had been fulfilled.

Wild with sorrow, they ran out of the palace on foot, not waiting for coaches, camels, or horses, and hurried hand in hand toward the castle where the seventh and kindest fairy lived.

The fairy saw them from her window, and came out to meet them.

'You need not tell me why you are so sad,' she said, 'for I know what has happened. You will never see your child again. Nor can you return to your palace, for my cruel sister has already surrounded it by a thick tangle of thorns and briars.'

'Oh, kind fairy,' cried the King and Queen, 'can you do

nothing to help us?'

'I have done all I can. And you have at least this comfort. When your daughter wakes, she will find her maids-of-honour, and her pages, and even her pet dogs and birds near her, for they have fallen into the same enchanted sleep as she, and when she opens her eyes they will open *theirs*.'

With this promise the poor King and Queen had to be content. They soon saw that the fairy had spoken truly, and that they could never cut their way through the great, tangled forest of thorns and briars which had suddenly sprung up round the palace where the Princess lay asleep. Very sorrowfully they made their way to the nearest of their other palaces, wishing that the fairy had sent *them* to sleep as well as the pages and the pet dogs and birds.

A hundred years passed, and nobody had tried to penetrate the thorn-forest, which had become a dense, tangled wilderness, dark, and mysterious, and strange.

Then, one fine morning, a Prince from a nearby country was out hunting, and in his eagerness he outstripped all his companions, and galloped so far that he found himself at last in a lonely valley which he did not remember to have seen before, and on the edge of a thick, gloomy wood. No one was in sight except an old woodcutter sitting on a tree-stump with his axe beside him.

'I am sure I do not know this place,' thought the Prince, 'I must certainly have lost my way. I wonder if there is a castle anywhere about, where I could get something to eat — for I am fearfully hungry!'

He beckoned to the woodcutter to come nearer, and, when he had come, he said, 'Good fellow, I have left my friends far behind, and it seems to me that I have lost my way. Is there a castle anywhere near here, where a hungry sportsman would be kindly received?'

The old man shook his head. 'There be no castles hereabouts, young Sir, nor no houses either. It is as lonely a piece o' country as any in the kingdom. My father, he *did* say there was a castle in that wood, and a sleeping Princess in it, too. But I don't heed those old tales, I don't. Nought but moonshine, says I!'

Now, in his childhood the Prince had heard a story of a Sleeping Beauty, but he had forgotten all about it until this moment. As he was a brave and gallant youth, and loved adventures, he determined to try to force his way through the knotted and tangled branches and find out for himself whether the story were really 'moonshine' or not. So he dismounted, tied his horse to a tree, and offered the woodcutter a piece of good red gold in exchange for his axe. The offer was quickly accepted, but the Prince soon found that he did not need the axe, for the moment he touched the knotted branches with his hand, they came unknotted and sprang apart as if to let him through.

Deeper and deeper the Prince pushed his way, all the briars and trailing creepers and matted thorns dividing before him, and after he had walked about a mile he reached a great and stately palace, with walls of coloured marble, and windows of crystal, and turrets of copper and gold. The door stood open, and so he walked boldly in. Everything was silent inside the palace, but nothing was faded, or dusty, or crumbling with age, though the Prince knew at once that the furniture must be at least a hundred years old, and some of it much older.

On tip-toe he passed from one beautiful room to another, some with walls of looking-glass, some with walls of mother-of-pearl, some with walls of ivory, till at last, in the very centre of the palace, he came to the room where the Beauty lay in her enchanted sleep. At either end of her golden bed sat a lady-in-waiting, as fast asleep as she. Across the threshold lay her page, with the lute in his hand upon which he had been playing when the spell began. At her feet slumbered a fluffy white dog, and in the silver cage by her pillow three little birds with gaily coloured plumes were dreaming, each with his head tucked under his wing.

The Prince could not look at anyone or at anything but the Princess. Her hair had grown, and grown, till it covered her from head to foot with a mantle more lovely than the richest cloth of gold. There was colour in her cheeks and on her lips, and as he dropped on one knee beside her, the Prince thought he could see a very faint movement of her long dark lashes.

Now, being a Prince and having heard the story of the Sleeping Beauty in his childhood, he knew exactly what to do. He bent forward and kissed her. Immediately the three little birds began to sing, and the little white dog began to bark, the ladies-in-waiting rubbed their eyes, the page sat up and went on with his playing at the point where he had left off a hundred years before. And the Princess opened her eyes, and held out her hand to the Prince. Somehow she understood, but all she could say was 'My prince!'

Hardly had they time to enjoy this wonderful moment when a new great happiness overwhelmed everyone — the King and Queen arrived from their other palace. The seventh and kindest fairy had, after all, laid her spell on them as well, and now they were reunited with their daughter. Great celebrations were immediately arranged for the wedding between the Princess and her Prince. Everywhere there was laughter and joy.

Bad Sir Brian Botany

Sir Brian had a battleaxe with great big knobs on;
    He went among the villagers and blipped them on the
        head.
On Wednesday and on Saturday, but mostly on the latter
        day,
    He called at all the cottages, and this is what he said:

    'I am Sir Brian!' *(ting-ling)*
      'I am Sir Brian!' *(rat-tat)*
    'I am Sir Brian, as bold as a lion —
      Take *that!* — and *that!* — and *that!*'

Sir Brian had a pair of boots with great big spurs on,
    A fighting pair of which he was particularly fond.
On Tuesday and on Friday, just to make the street look
        tidy,
He'd collect the passing villagers and kick them in the
        pond.

    'I am Sir Brian!' *(sper-lash!)*
      'I am Sir Brian!' *(sper-losh!)*
    'I am Sir Brian , as bold as a lion —
      Is anyone else for a wash?'

BAD SIR BRIAN BOTANY

Sir Brian woke one morning, and he couldn't find his
    battleaxe;
He walked into the village in his second pair of boots.
    He had gone a hundred paces, when the street was full
       of faces,

    And the villagers were round him with ironical salutes.
    'You are Sir Brian? Indeed!
       You are Sir Brian? Dear, Dear!
    You are Sir Brian, as bold as a lion?
       Delighted to meet you here!'

Sir Brian went on a journey, and he found a lot of
    duckweed:
They pulled him out and dried him, and they blipped
    him on the head.
They took him by the breeches, and they hurled him
    into ditches,
And they pushed him under waterfalls, and this is what
    they said:

    'You are Sir Brian — don't laugh,
       You are Sir Brian — don't cry;
    You are Sir Brian, as bold as a lion —
       Sir Brian, the lion, good-bye!'

BAD SIR BRIAN BOTANY

Sir Brian struggled home again, and chopped up his
    battleaxe,
Sir Brian took his fighting boots, and threw them in the
    fire.
He is quite a different person now he hasn't got his spurs
    on,
And he goes about the village as B. Botany, Esquire.
    'I am Sir Brian? Oh, *no!*
       I am Sir Brian? Who's he?
    I haven't got any title, I'm Botany —
       Plain Mr Botany (B).'

A A Milne

Milly-Molly-Mandy goes Errands

Once upon a time there was a little girl.

She had a Father, and a Mother, and a Grandpa, and a Grandma, and an Uncle, and an Aunty; and they all lived together in a nice white cottage with a thatched roof.

This little girl had short hair, and short legs, and short frocks (pink-and-white-striped cotton in summer, and red serge in winter). But her name wasn't short at all. It was Millicent Margaret Amanda. But Father and Mother and Grandpa and Grandma and Uncle and Aunty couldn't very well call out 'Millicent Margaret Amanda!' every time they wanted her, so they shortened it to 'Milly-Molly-Mandy,' which is quite easy to say.

Now everybody in the nice white cottage with the thatched roof had some particular job to do — even Milly-Molly-Mandy.

Father grew vegetables in the big garden by the cottage. Mother cooked the dinners and did the washing. Grandpa took the vegetables to market in his little pony-cart. Grandma knitted socks and mittens and nice warm woollies for them all. Uncle kept cows (to give them milk) and chickens (to give them eggs). Aunty sewed frocks and shirts for them, and did the sweeping and dusting.

And Milly-Molly-Mandy, what did she do?

Well, Milly-Molly-Mandy's legs were short, as I've told you, but they were very lively, just right for running errands. So Milly-Molly-Mandy was quite busy, fetching and carrying things, and taking messages.

One fine day Milly-Molly-Mandy was in the garden play-

ing with Toby the dog, when Father poked his head out
from the other side of a big row of beans, and said:

'Milly-Molly-Mandy, run down to Mr Moggs' cottage and
ask for the trowel he borrowed of me!'

So Milly-Molly-Mandy said 'Yes, Farver!' and ran in to
get her hat.

At the kitchen door was Mother, with a basket of eggs in
her hand. And when she saw Milly-Molly-Mandy she said:

'Milly-Molly-Mandy, run down to Mrs Moggs and give
her these eggs. She's got visitors.'

So Milly-Molly-Mandy said 'Yes, Muvver!' and took the
basket. 'Trowel for Farver, eggs for Muvver,' she thought to
herself.

Then Grandpa came up and said:

'Milly-Molly-Mandy, please get me a ball of string from
Miss Muggins' shop — here's the penny.'

So Milly-Molly-Mandy said 'Yes, Grandpa!' and took the
penny, thinking to herself, 'Trowel for Farver, eggs for
Muvver, string for Grandpa.'

As she passed through the kitchen Grandma, who was
sitting in her armchair knitting, said:

'Milly-Molly-Mandy, will you get me a skein of red wool?
Here's a sixpence.'

So Milly-Molly-Mandy said 'Yes, Grandma!' and took

the sixpence. 'Trowel for Farver, eggs for Muvver, string for Grandpa, red wool for Grandma,' she whispered to herself.

As she went into the passage Uncle came striding up in a hurry.

'Oh, Milly-Molly-Mandy,' said Uncle, 'run like a good girl to Mr Blunt's shop, and tell him I'm waiting for the chicken-feed he promised to send!'

So Milly-Molly-Mandy said 'Yes, Uncle!' and thought to herself, 'Trowel for Farver, eggs for Muvver, string for Grandpa, red wool for Grandma, chicken-feed for Uncle.'

As she got her hat off the peg Aunty called from the parlour where she was dusting:

'Is that Milly-Molly-Mandy? Will you get me a packet of needles, dear? Here's a penny!'

So Milly-Molly-Mandy said 'Yes, Aunty!' and took the penny, thinking to herself, 'Trowel for Farver, eggs for Muvver, string for Grandpa, red wool for Grandma, chicken-feed for Uncle, needles for Aunty, and I do hope there won't be anything more!'

But there was nothing else, so Milly-Molly-Mandy started out down the path. When she came to the gate Toby the dog capered up, looking very excited at the thought of a walk. But Milly-Molly-Mandy eyed him solemnly, and said:

'Trowel for Farver, eggs for Muvver, string for Grandpa, red wool for Grandma, chicken-feed for Uncle, needles for Aunty. No, Toby, you musn't come now, I've too much to think about. But I promise to take you for a walk when I come back!'

So she left Toby the other side of the gate, and set off down the road, with the basket and the pennies and the sixpence.

Presently she met a little friend, and the little friend said:

GRANDPA . GRANDMA . FATHER . MOTHER . UNCLE . AUNTY . MILLY-MOLLY-MANDY.

'Hello, Milly-Molly-Mandy! I've got a new see-saw! Do come on it with me!'

But Milly-Molly-Mandy looked at her solemnly and said:

'Trowel for Farver, eggs for Muvver, string for Grandpa, red wool for Grandma, chicken-feed for Uncle, needles for Aunty. No, Susan, I can't come now, I'm busy. But I'd like to come when I get back — after I've taken Toby for a walk.'

So Milly-Molly-Mandy went on her way with the basket and the pennies and the sixpence.

Soon she came to the Moggs' cottage.

'Please, Mrs Moggs, can I have the trowel for Farver? — and here are some eggs from Muvver!' she said.

Mrs Moggs was very much obliged indeed for the eggs, and fetched the trowel and a piece of seed-cake for Milly-Molly-Mandy's own self. And Milly-Molly-Mandy went on her way with the empty basket.

Next she came to Miss Muggins' little shop.

'Please, Miss Muggins, can I have a ball of string for Grandpa and a skein of red wool for Grandma?'

So Miss Muggins put the string and the wool into Milly-Molly-Mandy's basket, and took the penny and a sixpence in exchange. So that left Milly-Molly-Mandy with one penny. And Milly-Molly-Mandy couldn't remember what that penny was for.

'Sweeties, perhaps?' said Miss Muggins, glancing at the row of glass bottles on the shelf.

But Milly-Molly-Mandy shook her head.

'No,' she said, 'and it can't be chicken-feed for Uncle, because that would be more than a penny, only I haven't got to pay for it.'

'It must be sweeties!' said Miss Muggins.

'No,' said Milly-Molly-Mandy, 'but I'll remember soon. Good morning, Miss Muggins!'

So Milly-Molly-Mandy went on to Mr Blunt's, and gave

him Uncle's message, and then she sat down on the doorstep and thought what that penny could be for.

And she couldn't remember.

But she remembered one thing: 'It's for Aunty,' she thought, 'and I love Aunty.' And she thought for just a little while longer. Then suddenly she sprang up and went back to Miss Muggins's shop.

'I've remembered!' she said. 'It's for needles for Aunty!'

So Miss Muggins put the packet of needles into the basket, and took the penny, and Milly-Molly-Mandy set off for home.

'That's a good little messenger to remember all those things!' said Mother, when she got there. They were just going to begin dinner. 'I thought you were only going with my eggs!'

'She went for my trowel!' said Father.

'And my string!' said Grandpa.

'And my wool!' said Grandma.

'And my chicken-feed!' said Uncle.

'And my needles!' said Aunty.

Then they all laughed; and Grandpa, feeling in his pocket said:

'Well, here's another errand for you — go and get yourself some sweeties!'

So after dinner Toby had a nice walk and his mistress got her sweets. And then Milly-Molly-Mandy and little-friend-Susan had a lovely time on the see-saw, chatting and eating raspberry-drops, and feeling very happy and contented indeed.

Joyce Lankester Brisley

Pop and the Funny Bundle

'Hello, Pop,' said Tim.

The old blackbird was perched on the garden fence as usual, waiting for his breakfast.

All through the long hard winter Tim had fed the wild birds with bread, crumbled and moistened, adding sultanas for sugar and not forgetting the fat they needed so much to keep them warm. There was always a lump of suet hanging over the bird table.

Now it was summer and the syringa tree was a canopy of white and the roses filled the air with perfume. Almost the only interested customers among the bird population were the very old and the very young.

Of course there were always the starlings. People said they were very greedy, but Mummy, who knew best, said this was because they were so energetic.

Pop had been coming to their garden to be fed for nearly a year now and had become very cheeky. He would take sultanas out of Tim's hand. He would follow Tim to any garden down the road where Tim went to play and sit on a fence or tree and call to him, as if he was telling him it was time to come home.

Today Pop seemed fidgety. He flew down to the path but kept flying back to the fence. When he came down to the path again he would not approach.

'What's the matter, Pop?' asked Tim. 'Is there a nasty cat about?'

Tim didn't really think cats were nasty, but he knew birds did. The old blackbird looked this way and that, but he didn't come any nearer.

POP AND THE FUNNY BUNDLE

Suddenly another bird flew down from the fence, plop, beside Pop. Such a funny lump of dusty brown feathers, it was, with a beak of no particular colour. From this Tim knew it must be a young bird, or its beak would be yellow, like Pop's, for it was certainly a blackbird. It sat there in a heap with eyes half closed.

Tim turned and hurried indoors, but quietly. You never made a noise when birds were about or they'd fly off.

'Mummy!' he called. 'Pop's brought such a funny bundle.'

'A bundle?' repeated his mother, smiling. 'A bundle of what?'

'A bundle of bird,' said Tim.

His mother came out with him and looked.

'It's a fledgling,' she said. 'I think it's hurt its leg. Perhaps it fell out of the nest.'

'Can it be Pop's baby?' asked Tim.

He had no need to ask what a fledgling was for he knew it was a young bird ready to fly.

'I should think so. Pop wants us to feed him, don't you Pop?'

The old blackbird whistled and ducked his head for all the world as if he was saying 'yes'. Then he picked up a sultana and gave it to the fledgling. In a few moments the young bird was feeding itself.

'I don't like the look of Pop today,' said Tim's mother. 'He's moulting too heavily and his eyes are not as bright as they should be.'

'Perhaps he's sick?' suggested Tim.

'I think he's just old,' said his mother.

When the two birds had had enough to eat they flew away, the young one looking much more lively.

'I shall call that one Bundle,' said Tim as they went indoors.

The next morning when Tim went out to feed the birds,

it was raining hard. He had his mac and wellingtons on so he was all right.

There was only one bird waiting. It was not Pop. It was Bundle, all hunched up and miserable as he looked yesterday.

'Cheer up, Bundle,' said Tim. 'Where's Pop?'

But the young blackbird couldn't tell him.

Tim threw down a few sultanas, then dropped them one by one through the garden doorway into the dry corridor. Then he stepped back and watched. Bundle hopped in, wobbling a bit on his bad leg. He ate all the sultanas. Then he hopped out again and took off awkwardly, managing to reach first the fence and then the syringa tree.

He came twice a day after that and soon his leg was mended. But there was no sign of Pop.

One day in late summer Tim was watching television when he heard a faint sound. He looked down and there, on the carpet, was a blackbird, its head going from side to side, its bright eyes fixed on the moving figures on the screen.

Very quietly Tim got up and crept into the kitchen.

'Come and see who is watching television, Mummy!' he cried excitedly. 'You'll never guess!'

When Tim's mother saw that it was Bundle she stood there laughing and amazed.

'I've never seen anything like that,' she said.

She went into the kitchen and fetched some sultanas. Then she laid down a trail from the sitting-room along the corridor to the garden door.

'If we frighten Bundle,' she explained to Tim,' he may hurt himself badly by flying into the walls and furniture. Now, I'll throw him a sultana.'

Bundle was still watching the moving screen when he noticed the sultana land near him. He ate it up and looked for more. He ate the next one and the next, walking, flat-footed, into the corridor and out through the garden door.

Then Tim and his mother stood and laughed together while Bundle flew away, full of sultanas.

'If only Pop could have seen him!' said Tim, and became rather thoughtful. 'What do you think has happened to Pop, Mummy?'

'I think he felt he was too old to make a good job of being a father any more, Tim,' said his mother, 'so he brough Bundle to you to care for.'

Tim liked this idea very much for it meant he was some-one to be trusted.

Martha Robinson

Queen Maggie

There was once a queen called Maggie, who was married to a king named Charlie.

Charlie enjoyed being a king. He liked sitting on his throne; wearing long robes and purple cloaks; nodding ever so slightly when people bowed to him; and counting his bags of gold and silver on a Friday afternoon. He also enjoyed banging on the dinner gong and when the cook came puffing up the stairs — saying to her, 'I'LL have my dinner now Mrs Pudding.'

Maggie, however, HATED having to behave like a queen. She hated sitting on the throne, and refused to do it most times. She hated her purple cloak and would only wear it on the king's birthday. She loathed people bowing to her, and if anyone did she would say to them,

'Get up! You'll make yourself dizzy down there. Silly!'

'My Flower!' complained the king, wearily, 'you really must make an effort to behave in a manner more befitting a queen.'

'What?' said Maggie.

'It's hopeless, isn't it!' said the king to the ceiling.

One Friday afternoon when the king was counting out his money, he let out a great cry of dismay. Maggie came racing into the room.

'What is it Charlie? Have you sat on a snake?' She knew the king disliked snakes.

'There's a bee on the window, is there?' she flapped the curtains furiously to frighten it away.

'I know! — you've got a tummy ache. It was those dreadful meat-balls Mrs Pudding gave us for lunch.'

'For goodness sake, Maggie!' said the king, when he could get a word in edgeways, 'it's got nothing to do with snakes or bees or meat-balls, it's to do with money. We've only got ONE bag of gold left.'

'Ah, is that all?' said Maggie, wishing it had been something more exciting than that. 'What a fuss about nothing.'

'About nothing! Really my Petal, how do you suppose I shall pay the servants, or Mrs Pudding?'

'I'LL pay Mrs Pudding,' decided the queen. She liked Mrs Pudding best of all. 'I'll sell my crown.'

'You certainly shan't,' stormed the king, indignantly. He knew that Maggie's crown was the only part of the Royal Regalia his wife DID like to wear.

'You certainly shan't,' he said again, because he liked saying it.

'O.K.' said Maggie, 'if you don't like that idea, Sausage, I'll organise a jumble sale.'

'You certainly shan't,' said the king for the third time. 'You . . . ' But Maggie was half way down the palace corridor, singing, ta ra, ta ra, ta ra, TA RA, because she had the feeling Charlie was trying to say something else.

As soon as she reached the Royal Bedroom, she bounced up and down on the bed, laughing, 'I'm going to have a Jumble Sale! A Super Rumble Jumble Sale!'

She rang all the people she knew.

The ones who could knit.

The ones who could sew.

The ones who could make peppermint fudge.

The ones who could draw donkeys for stick-the-tail-on games. And Mr Billy Jolly because he was absolutely marvellous at organising Lucky Dips.

They all said, 'yes', of course. No one ever says 'no' to a queen.

QUEEN MAGGIE

After that Maggie raced downstairs to the kitchen calling, 'Mrs Pudding? Mrs Pudding! I'm going to have a Jumble Sale because the king hasn't much money left. I want you to make a hundred and ninety-three jam tarts, sixty-eight eclairs, and a couple of thousand sandwiches — meat paste and eggy ones will do fine.'

'I . . . . ' began Mrs Pudding, turning pasty.

But Maggie had already gone to town to buy tables and garden chairs.

The following afternoon, King Charlie had hardly done three hours throne-sitting-duty (and no one had been in to bow to him) when he heard the most DREADFUL COMMOTION in the garden.

'It's an INVASION!' he gasped. It MUST be!'

Then he saw Maggie's Jumble Sale,

'That queen is crazy!' he muttered. 'Well, I'm not going out there for a thousand pounds (even though I am short of money). I'm going up to bed and put my ears under the pillow until it's all over.'

And he did. Pretty cross he was really.

In the garden everyone was having a lovely time. The shopkeepers in the town wondered why no one was coming into their shops. It was, after all, a Saturday afternoon.

'Haven't you heard?' cried some of the passers-by. 'The queen is holding a Super Rumble Jumble Sale.'

'Is she?' said the butcher, 'I didn't know.'

'Nor I,' said the baker.

'Nor I,' said the candlestick-maker.

And they drew down their blinds and went to it.

There was a big crowd round the Donkey Game, because the Vicar was winning over and over again and getting lots of prizes.

'Hem!' coughed Maggie, staring very hard at him until she caught sight of one twinkly eye peeping through a hole in the blind-fold.

'Mustn't cheat must we!' she said, poking the Vicar in the tummy and teasing, 'tut tut, who's a naughty old Vicar?'

Suddenly the Vicar didn't feel like playing any more and he hurried off towards the tea-tent.

'Oooh! fancy that!' said the crowd, 'and him a vicar!'

Maggie was selling ice-cream now. The queue was getting longer and longer. This was because for every ice-cream Maggie sold, she ate one herself. Some of the people who were at the back of the queue (nearly a mile long now) grew tired and went away to try their fortune in Mr Billy Jolly's Lucky Dip.

All this time the king could not sleep at all. He kept slipping his ears out of the pillow to hear if the DREADFUL COMMOTION had stopped, but it hadn't.

'It's even DREADFULLER I think,' moaned the king.

And then he said, 'Well blow me! I AM the king after all. And it IS my garden. I'll go down and stop them. I'll jolly well stop 'em. Cheek!' he said, as he hurried downstairs.

'Where's the Queen!?' he bellowed to Mr Billy Jolly.

'Don't know, Your Majesty,' stuttered Mr Billy Jolly.

'And I suppose you don't know either that your standing on my best pansies? Move man! or I'll stuff you into your own bran tub.'

The king wasn't really a violent man. He just felt EXASPERATED this particular afternoon. He went stamping round the grounds looking for Maggie. He wouldn't buy a pair of bootees for his grandson, or a stuffed hippopotamus, or even a bag of peppermint fudge, which just proves how cross he was.

Then he came across the ice-cream queue, and Maggie at the top of it.

'THERE you are!' exploded the king, red in the face with crossness.

'Hullo love,' said Maggie, giving a little boy an extra big splosh of ice-cream on account of him being only four. 'D'you want an ice-cream?'

'No I do NOT!' snapped Charlie. 'And I don't think it's fitting for a queen to be seen licking ice-cream in public.'

'Why not, Dear Heart?' asked the Queen, mildly.

'Because . . . . because, well just BECAUSE!' Charlie couldn't think.

Maggie said, 'Hold the money a minute will you whilst I serve the candlestick-maker. He's been waiting simply ages.'

King Charlie took hold of the ice-cream money and it weighed him nearly down to the ground.

'Good heavens!' he thought. 'My whiskers! My best Sunday crown! What a lot of money!'

Maggie finished serving the candlestick-maker, and began to take off her apron.

'All right,' she said, 'if my Super Rumble Jumble Sale is really upsetting you I'll tell everyone it's time to go home.'

'No no!' said Charlie. 'Let us not be hasty. After all, my people are having such a lovely time it would be a shame to send them all home. Do I LOOK like an old fuddy duddy king?'

'Of course you don't look like an old fuddy duddy king,' cried Maggie, giving her husband a huge hug and an ice-cream. 'You look very handsome. And terribly grand. And most enormously important.'

'Yes,' agreed the king.

'And d'you know what I think?'

'No,' said the king.

'I think everybody would like to shake hands with you — 5p a go.'

'Do you think so, My Petal?'

'I certainly do!' said the queen.

So King Charlie sent Mr Diggup, the gardener, helter-skeltering into the palace to fetch his throne, and he said to him, 'Put it there, by the pansies, Mr Diggup.'

And he sent Mrs Pudding waddle waddling into the kitchen to fetch an empty biscuit tin into which he put the money. And he said, 'Put it down here, and TRY not to squash any more pansies.'

Then of course ABSOLUTELY EVERYBODY wanted to shake hands with the king. And they thought 5p was very cheap to do it and excellent value for money. It was nearly dark by the time the VERY LAST PERSON had finished shaking the king's hand and there were a lot of squashed pansies around the palace gardens, and a lot of half-eaten ice-creams and pieces of sandwiches, and the ear off a stuffed hippopotamus and one knitted bootee some-one had dropped . . . . a month's tidying up for Mr Diggup. But King Charlie was happy. He had lots and lots of money again.

'I LIKE Rumble Jumble Sales,' he said sleepily.

'I knew all the time you would,' Queen Maggie said.

And they had six more ice-creams each and then they went to bed.

Margaret Stuart Barry

The Mad Gardener's Song

He thought he saw an Elephant,
   That practised on a fife:
He looked again, and found it was
   A letter from his wife.
'At length I realize,' he said,
   'The bitterness of Life!'

He thought he saw a Buffalo
   Upon the chimney-piece:
He looked again, and found it was
   His Sister's Husband's Niece.
'Unless you leave this house,' he said,
   'I'll send for the Police!'

He thought he saw a Rattlesnake
    That questioned him in Greek:
He looked again, and found it was
    The Middle of Next Week.

'The one thing I regret,' he said,
  'Is that it cannot speak!'

He thought he saw a Banker's Clerk
  Descending from the bus:
He looked again, and found it was
  A Hippopotamus:
'If this should stay to dine,' he said,
  'There won't be much for us!'

He thought he saw a Kangaroo
  That worked a coffee-mill:
He looked again, and found it was
  A Vegetable-Pill.
'Were I to swallow this,' he said,
  'I should be very ill!'

He thought he saw a Coach-and-Four
  That stood beside his bed:

He looked again, and found it was
    A Bear without a Head.
'Poor thing,' he said, 'poor silly thing!
    It's waiting to be fed!'

He thought he saw an Albatross
    That fluttered round the lamp:

THE MAD GARDENER'S SONG

He looked again, and found it was
    A Penny-Postage-Stamp.
'You'd best be getting home,' he said:
    'The nights are very damp!'

He thought he saw a Garden-Door
    That opened with a key:
He looked again, and found it was
    A Double Rule of Three:
'And all its mystery,' he said,
    'Is clear as day to me!'

He thought he saw an Argument
    That proved he was the Pope:
He looked again, and found it was
    A Bar of Mottled Soap.
'A fact so dread,' he faintly said,
    'Extinguishes all hope!'

Lewis Carroll

Jabberwocky

'Twas brillig, and the slithy toves
   Did gyre and gimble in the wabe:
All mimsy were the borogoves,
   And the mome raths outgrabe.

'Beware the Jabberwock, my son!
   The jaws that bite, the claws that catch!
Beware the Jubjub bird, and shun
   The frumious Bandersnatch!'

He took his vorpal sword in hand:
   Long time the manxome foe he sought—
So rested he by the Tumtum tree,
   And stood awhile in thought.

And, as in uffish thought he stood,
   The Jabberwock, with eyes of flame,
Came whiffling through the tulgey wood,
   And burbled as it came!

One, two! One, two! And through and through
   The vorpal blade went snicker-snack!
He left it dead, and with its head
   He went galumphing back.

'And hast thou slain the Jabberwock?
   Come to my arms, my beamish boy!
O frabjous day! Callooh! Callay!'
   He chortled in his joy.

'Twas brillig, and the slithy toves
   Did gyre and gimble in the wabe:
All mimsy were the borogoves,
   And the mome raths outgrabe.

Lewis Carroll

More Beaver Books

We hope you have enjoyed this Beaver Book. Here are some of the other titles:

Read Me Another Story Traditional nursery rhymes and fairy tales mix with new and original material in this delightful collection suitable for the youngest readers or for reading aloud. Selected and edited by Frank Waters

Over and Over Again A Beaver original. A superb collection of poems and songs, old and new, for the very youngest children, compiled by Barbara Ireson and Christopher Rowe and illustrated by Russell Coulson

Rhyme Time A Beaver original. Over 200 poems specially chosen by Barbara Ireson to introduce younger readers to the pleasures of reading verse. This lively collection is illustrated throughout by Lesley Smith

Wilberforce, Detective A funny and exciting story for younger readers in which Wilberforce the whale is called upon to protect the Crown Jewels! Written by Leslie Coleman and illustrated by John Laing

These and many other Beavers are available at your local bookshop or newsagent, or can be ordered direct from: Hamlyn Paperback Cash Sales, PO Box 11, Falmouth, Cornwall TR10 9EN. Send a cheque or postal order, made payable to The Hamlyn Publishing Group, for the price of the book plus postage at the following rates:

UK: 22p for the first book plus 10p a copy for each extra book ordered to a maximum of 92p;

BFPO and EIRE: 22p for the first book plus 10p a copy for the next 6 books and thereafter 4p a book;

OVERSEAS: 30p for the first book and 10p for each extra book.

New Beavers are published every month and if you would like the *Beaver Bulletin*, which gives a complete list of books and prices, including new titles, send a large stamped addressed envelope to:

Beaver Bulletin
The Hamlyn Group
Astronaut House
Feltham
Middlesex TW14 9AR

375803